LETTERS FROM THE CORRUGATED CASTLE

A Novel of Gold Rush California,
1850–1852

JOAN W. BLOS

GINEE SEO BOOKS
ATHENEUM BOOKS FOR YOUNG READERS
NEW YORK LONDON TORONTO SYDNEY

Atheneum Books for Young Readers
An imprint of Simon & Schuster Children's Publishing Division
1230 Avenue of the Americas, New York, New York 10020
Book design by Michael McCartney
The text for this book is set in New Century Schoolbook.
Manufactured in the United States of America
First Edition
10 9 8 7 6 5 4 3 2 1
CIP data for this book is available from the Library of Congress.
ISBN-13: 978-0-689-87077-4
ISBN-10: 0-689-87077-9

CLICHÉS BECOME CLICHÉS
BECAUSE THEY ARE CONVENIENT,
PARSIMONIOUS, AND TRUE.
THIS BOOK IS DEDICATED
TO MY HUSBAND, PETER,
WITHOUT WHOM IT WOULD NEVER
HAVE BEEN POSSIBLE.

Contents

CHAPTER I

Eldora

AUGUST 5, 1850 – NOVEMBER 18, 1850

*No story begins entirely of itself.
There is a story behind each and
every story, and behind that story
there is yet another.*

JOHN HALL, TRAVELS IN THE WEST

San Francisco, California
Monday, August 5, 1850

Dear Cousin Sallie,

I begin with words I never thought to write: I am not an orphan! Never mind that we have believed this to be so since I was first brought to live with Aunt and Uncle (not my real aunt and uncle as you well know).

Yesterday Aunt received a letter from a woman who lives in San Pedro, which is in the Salinas Valley, some three days' journey hence. The woman, whose name is Señora Elisabeth Ramos, believes me to be her daughter! She tells that she did not die of cholera in Panama as has been understood to be the case. She has been twice widowed. Her first husband was my father. Her second husband died shortly after the ending of the war with Mexico. They did not have any children. So I am her only daughter, her only child. She hopes that she may

3

=

visit when she is next in San Francisco.

Aunt told me this morning that she and Uncle are agreed that when she replies to Mrs. Ramos, she will say only that we have received her news, rejoice at her well-being, and will welcome a visit. "And," Aunt said, looking at me directly, "until that happens, Eldora, we will speak no more of her letter nor expend ourselves on conjecture."

I was greatly curious but asking questions would have been of no use. It has always been Aunt's way not to spend time in thinking on matters until they require attention. Uncle is more reflective and, in that regard, I am more like him. It will hardly surprise you, therefore, that he was the one to join me, over the next several days, in wondering how my mother—if indeed she *is* my mother—learned of my whereabouts. Nor will it surprise you to hear that when Uncle and I speculated aloud as to whether I resemble her in appearance, Aunt busied herself at the cookstove and had nothing to say on the matter.

It is twelve weeks since we said our farewells, four since we arrived in this place, three since our iron house was erected, and two since we saw our first fire. We are told that fires are quite common here, many dwellings being made of tent canvas or hastily constructed of wood. I am glad we have an iron house.

We stayed in a hotel while awaiting the walls, doors, windows, and so forth needed for the construction of our house. These necessary parts were sent from New York City but, having been ordered before we left New Bedford, were not too long in arriving. As soon as the shipment containing them arrived, Uncle engaged a man to assist in assembling our new home. It took only two days to complete it. Aunt's cookstove required nearly four days! It was also sent, disassembled, from New York City, and it was our good fortune that it arrived at nearly the same time as the house.

The furnishings are few: a table that serves many purposes, a rocking chair, several straight chairs, shelves for Uncle's books, and a bed for Aunt and Uncle. Aunt has curtained one corner to form a sleeping place for me. A small table next to my bed holds a basin and a pitcher. A chamber pot is stored under the bed. All very convenient!

Although the price is dear, we have purchased some few items in addition to the kettle, fry pan, coffee pot, and tableware we brought with us. A well-made broom pleased Aunt especially, and also a bucket of good size. Uncle has taken to referring to our new home as our corrugated castle! It is small but quite comfortable.

We three remain in excellent health although we are surrounded by much illness. The cholera is the worst of it. Many people arrive in weakened condition due to the travail they have endured merely to reach this place. In that regard it does not seem to matter whether one travels overland or, as we did, by sea.

I trust that you also are well, and hope to hear that this is indeed the case. Has Baby Emily got her first tooth? She is the cunningest baby I have ever seen. I liked so much to hold her and make her smile. It is hard to imagine how she will look with teeth! I think it would make *me* smile!

We have not yet received any letters, so you can appreciate our concern and curiosity. Are you addressing letters to San Francisco, California, and prepaying them? It appears this is necessary for their secure receipt. I hope I am the first to receive a letter and that it comes from you!

I hope I will soon be able to tell you about my mother's visit if Mrs. Ramos is indeed my mother. Aunt cautions me that I must not place all my hopes on it.

With greatest affection,
Eldora

San Francisco, California
Monday, August 12, 1850

Dear Cousin Sallie,

Aunt has received another letter from Mrs. Ramos. Because of her business, the nature of which we do not know as yet, she will be in this city in a few weeks' time and hopes to call on us then. She is quite certain that I am her daughter but she wrote very little about herself, or how she found me, or why she believes she is my mother. In consequence of which we are more curious than ever! I grow more impatient with each passing day but Aunt worries that a mistake has been made and that the woman who wrote to us is not my mother after all. "How will we *know*?" she asks. To which Uncle replies in his steadying way, "We will know, and so will she."

The letter from Mrs. Ramos was posted in Monterey. It came with the mail ship but only after considerable delay due to contrary winds. It was the only letter we received.

While waiting for the mail to be distributed, Uncle met a man named Mr. Hall and his son. The son, who is traveling with him, is named Luke. He is a good deal taller than I am and already has a low voice. His father mentioned that Luke has only recently passed his fourteenth birthday so he is older than I am, but only by a year. Luke is able to travel with his father because he no longer attends school. Why this is so was not explained. I could tell that Uncle was curious, but he did not ask!

Mr. Hall is a newspaper writer from the state of Michigan. He intends to write about California's cities, people, and gold mines. The newspaper for the town where he lives will publish his dispatches. He says that every one is eager to read about California, as every one is hoping to come here or they know someone who is here already. Mr. Hall told Uncle that Millfield, which is where he lives, and also the next town over, are short of doctors, lawyers, and shopkeepers because they have all left for California!

Uncle says that he and Mr. Hall have discovered

that they are very much in agreement about books, shipping companies, and political matters. Aunt laughed when he told us. She was certain, she said, that the last was most important. Then she added that she hoped this new friend would pay us a visit so she might form her own impression. Uncle said he had already made the suggestion, and hoped that the son would come too. Evidently the idea met with Mr. Hall's approval for he came today and his son came with him!

Mr. Hall is friendly and can be quite funny. But if the son stays at the hotel the next time his father decides to visit he will not be very much missed. He did not seem much interested in what others were saying and when asked a question said little more than "Yes, sir" and "No, sir" in reply.

Aunt served slices of the bread that she had made only that morning, and with it honey we had brought with us. She used the China tea—bought here—for the first time. Mr. Hall exclaimed at the bread and protested her generosity with the honey. But Luke spread his bread with several spoonfuls of it, and licked his fingers as boldly as you please. Aunt said nothing at the time. But after they left she commented on his unmannerly behavior. Uncle said he thought that Luke was a very unhappy boy. I wonder why Uncle believes this to be the case. I did not know boys could be unhappy.

Aunt is calling. I will end this letter now and write more tomorrow or the next day.

Eldora

The *Millfield Herald* is pleased to announce that Mr. John Hall, well known to residents of this city, has consented to furnish readers of this publication with accounts of his travels and impressions while visiting California and its goldfields. He intends to remain there for some months.

(Signed)
SHEM PERKINS, *Editor*

San Francisco, California
Tuesday, September 3, 1850

Dear Cousin Sallie,

I think you will laugh when I tell you that I have
made a friend who does not speak English and
appears to be no more than five years old! Possibly
she is older as *Mexicanos* tend to be small even
when they are grown.

This afternoon Aunt had gone down to Portsmouth Square (which is the central plaza) and I had
completed the lesson Uncle set for me. As is usually
the case in California, it was quite pleasant outside. I
was seated on the empty packing box that Aunt and I
use as a dooryard bench. Seated there, one can see up
the street as well as down. On one day we will admire
the clothesline a neighbor has strung from a corner
of her house to a sturdy pole; another day we will
laugh to see a household's entire washload displayed
spread-eagle flat on the canvas roof of their tent.

Today, my attention was captured by a small girl, with the blackest hair you ever saw, as she came up the street. She was looking with frank curiosity at the houses along the way—the canvas tents, an iron house larger than ours, and several dwellings of wood that boast framed windows.

I had the impression that our street represented quite a novelty to the little girl, and perhaps it did. Once, I recalled, Uncle had described coming upon a portion of the city where most of the houses were small adobes. It was a rather short distance from this area, perhaps only a ten- or fifteen-minute walk, but seemed to belong to another world. Most of the residents, he had added, appeared to be *Mexicanos*. So perhaps that explained not only the child's curiosity but also the cut of her long black skirt and embroidered cotton blouse.

As she came closer, I saw that she was cradling some roughly knotted cloth with twigs sticking out on either side. Its identity puzzled me at first. But the tender way she sang to it showed it to be a well-loved doll. The child halted when she came to our gate, stared at me with curiosity equal to mine, and quickly looked away. I looked at her, smiled, and patted the space beside me. As an invitation, it was understood and accepted.

For a few minutes neither of us spoke. When the silence became uncomfortably long, I offered the information that we were from New Bedford, Massachusetts, and that my name was Eldora. The child listened carefully but when she spoke it was to say, "No English."

A few minutes later she touched my hair with one finger and said, "*Dorado.*" Thinking she meant to say my name, which I had just revealed, I corrected her. I had not guessed her intention, however. She sighed deeply as if despairing at my stupidity, and shook her head, no.

Then she ventured to touch my hair again and quietly but clearly repeated what she had said. Next, she pointed to her own hair and said, "*Negro.*" Then she pointed to herself and said, "Lucia," and finally, she pointed to me and said, very clearly, "Eldora." At this I laughed aloud for the sheer joy of understanding our exchange. Following her example, I spoke my name and hers and the colors of her hair and mine. Then a new thought struck me. Pointing to the doll she carried, I asked the doll's name. Lucia looked puzzled at this and I knew I would have to try again.

"My name," I said, pointing at myself, "Eldora. Your name: Lucia. And"—here I pointed at the doll—"her name?"

"No name," she said.

"No name?" I repeated, and Lucia nodded. So, from that moment on, No-Name was the name of the doll.

We were very pleased to have begun a friendship in this way and cared not at all for the differences between us. Only a short while later a young *Mexicano*, broader in the shoulders than Luke but not as tall, came up the street. He stopped when he saw us and shook a finger at Lucia. He was speaking Spanish so I did not understand the words except for "*madre*," which he said several times and quite sharply. It was clear that she was to come with him at once and that her mother was vexed. Lucia stood up quickly, put the doll under her arm, and bade me, "*Adiós.*" I said the same to her, following it with, "Good-bye."

I think it was her brother that came to find her. He seemed not surprised, just cross, that she had wandered into the neighborhood of the *Americanos*. Evidently this was not the first time she had done so and he had been sent to look for her.

After Lucia and her brother left, I remained seated for a while and that was when one of our neighbors came hurrying out of her house. She lives only two houses west of ours and she was in such haste that she was still drying her hands on her apron as she came toward me.

"It is not good to play with *Mexicanos*," she said. "Dirt. Disease. Also, they are thieves. I am quite certain your mother would not approve."

"Perhaps you have seen me with Mrs. Holt," I said. "But she is not my mother."

If my intention had been to discomfort her, the expression of dismay that came over her face showed that I had succeeded. I knew I owed her an apology. But, rankled by the way she had spoken of Lucia, I was disinclined to give the woman the least information. I just sat there and she just stood there.

After a few minutes, during which neither one of us spoke, she shrugged, looked at me crossly, and walked back to her house which she then entered. I suppose it was rude of me to behave as I did and she will probably regard me as a hateful child forever. That is not so bad. But if she tells others about me it could cause trouble for Uncle and I would be sorry.

Uncle is working very hard to start a school here. As you know he is very much influenced by Mr. Alcott and his writings, and Uncle intends his school to be one where students learn to trust themselves beyond the teachings of books. Thus, he says, he will not so much instruct the students as guide them in their learning. He is firm in his beliefs but these ideas are new ideas, not yet widely held. For this reason, he has told me more than once, it is important that our neighbors think well of us and trust him as a teacher.

I hope I will make a better impression on the next neighbor who talks to me.

Ever and fondly,
Eldora

San Francisco, California
Thursday, September 12, 1850

Dear Cousin Sallie,

We had thought that my mother would come this second week of September, and I had already begun counting the days and imagining what we would say to one another. "How do you do? I am very glad to meet you"? No, that would not be right! Or, "Oh my dear daughter! How tall you have grown!" No, that is what relatives say when they have not seen you in a while. This will be my *mother*, and she has not seen me since I was three years old. The worst thing I wonder about is whether she will like me. The next worst thing is that I might not like *her*.

Now she has written that she must postpone her visit until October so I must wait another whole month before my questions even begin to be answered. I can see that I was foolish to set my heart on her visit. Aunt says that in each of her letters my mother writes of her happiness at having found me. But maybe that is not altogether true and probably she is not as disappointed as I am that her visit is delayed.

I fear that my doubts and disappointments have made a tedious letter, and so, to spare you, I will turn my thoughts to some thing else.

New neighbors have replaced the woman who scolded me for playing with Lucia. When Uncle told us that she had gone to join her husband in the diggings I said I felt sorry for her husband, having such an unpleasant person as his wife. Aunt said, "Really, Eldora!" But her voice did not match her words and I think she agrees with me though she will never say so.

The new neighbors used to live in Ohio. They traveled overland, a long and difficult journey. The wife told us that they had painted the words GOING TO SEE THE ELEPHANT on one side of their wagon and BOUND FOR CALIFORNIA on the other.

I understood about "Bound for California" but not about the elephant. After they left I asked Uncle what elephant they were going to see, which made him laugh. It wasn't about a real elephant, he explained, just a way of saying they were on their way to a rare and unusual sight. Whatever their hopes had been, their travels were difficult.

They had very little water and not enough food. While they were crossing the plains, one and then another of their oxen died—gave out, as they said. For a brief while, with herself pulling the wagon and her husband pushing, they tried to continue on their way. But they were weakened by all they had been through and they were in mortal fear that one or the other of them would not survive the journey. Finally, they left the wagon and just about every thing they had brought from their home, and continued on foot.

"Now, that was some punkins!" the wife said. "Me in my condition and my husband worn out from walking half the way we'd come so as to spare the oxen—little good it did them, poor beasts—and us getting here with never a skillet nor a broom and no rocking chair, neither, for me to sit in, nursing the baby, when the baby comes."

That is the way she talks, with many things run together. She said one good thing had come of it all, which is that her husband has decided to take up lawyering, which is what he did in the States, instead of mining. Then she took her leave and said she was pleased to have made our acquaintance, though we hadn't done more than shake hands and say our names.

We met the husband, who does not talk very much, the next day. Uncle said maybe that is because his wife does not leave him much room! "Now, Edward," Aunt said, using the same voice she uses some times in scolding me, "you can tell she is good spirited, and good hearted."

I think that is true.

A few days later a divorced woman—the first divorced woman I ever met—set up a tent on the other side of us. She has twin daughters who are just learning to walk, and a girl not much older. Maybe she will let me help take care of them! I would like that because it would remind me of Baby Emily. When I asked Aunt why they had gotten divorced, Aunt said she had no idea, was not about to inquire, and I should not do so either.

I surely do not intend to inquire, as Aunt put it, but I will tell you if I find out. I wonder how it would feel to have parents who are not dead but who do not live in the same family.

These days the harbor, which we can see from our street, is so filled with masts it looks like a floating forest. Every day, more ships arrive until you have to wonder how they are all able to anchor safely.

But it is not just the harbor that is crowded and bustling. New buildings are going up all the time and at such a rate that I expect San Francisco does not look at all the way it did in any pictures any one might have seen before leaving home just a few months ago. Hotels and rooming houses are so full it is hard to find rooms! Until they can find more permanent accommodations or put up some sort of dwelling of their own, many people use the ships on which they came as floating hotels.

When the passengers disembark, you can see that the men are laden with the tools and supplies they suppose they will need for mining. But there is always some thing they lack and are obliged to purchase here. In consequence, San Francisco is busier than ever. The prices are high, Uncle says, but it makes no difference. Every one who comes here has got gold fever and they all believe they will be very rich very soon and they spend what they have. The women just look tired. There are not so many of them as men and most of them have small children.

Yesterday Lucia came with her doll *and* her brother! He speaks more English than she does, although not a lot. His name is Miguel and he works on the wharves helping to unload the ships. He says he is paid good money (I think he means a lot of money) and that it is good he is strong. Although, as I have said, some passengers stay on the ships until they are ready to go to the diggings, others look for rooms in the city. Once they have found lodgings, they are happy to pay Miguel to carry their things to the hotel or rooming house.

Mr. Hall and his son have called again. When they appeared at our door, Uncle was engaged in responding to a letter that he was glad to have received but he quickly stoppered the ink and laid his pen aside. Mr. Hall soon revealed that he too had been rewarded by the mail ship's arrival. A letter from his wife had put his mind at ease as to her well-being.

Mr. Hall is the first writer I have ever met and that is even more interesting than having a neighbor who is divorced. I hope he comes again.

Uncle asked Luke if he would be attending school while here. Luke said he has left schooling behind him and that mining is his present intention. As you can imagine, Uncle was not very pleased by this answer. Most of the miners we have seen are a good bit older than Luke and seem a rather rough lot. I wonder if Luke has noticed. I wonder if Mr. Hall knows.

I hope you will write soon. Tell me all you can about what is happening in New Bedford. Does your sister still admire Samuel D. so much? I hope she has changed her mind. Is Baby Emily able to walk yet? Do you have a good teacher? To receive a letter from you will give me much pleasure.

Eldora

SAN FRANCISCO:
FIRST IMPRESSIONS
BY JOHN HALL

I arrived in San Francisco with the expectation that I would find a city of canvas tents and improvised wooden shacks. Instead, I was greeted by brick buildings, some of them three and four storeys high, and a central plaza known as Portsmouth Square. Surrounding it are wooden tables where doctors, lawyers, accountants, and diverse others ply their trades from morning until night. The post office is located on the square and when a mail ship arrives, long lines of persons eager for news from home form at its windows. I am told that those who can afford to do so will pay others who are less fortunate to await the distribution of mail and, on their behalf, claim such letters and parcels as may be addressed to them.

The city is growing rapidly and the cause is not hard to discover. Gold fever is as contagious as any malady and it has brought untold numbers of persons to the area. It was spread by stories brought back by sailors who visited this coast, by the writings of my estimable colleague, Mr. Bayard Taylor, and by the excited reports of miners. Rumors of lucky strikes abound, and not a few miners boast of having enriched themselves by hundreds of dollars in a single day's labor. One of the more unusual tales describes a lady who swept the earthen floor of her cabin and came on a goodly amount of gold.

With stories such as this making their way back to the eastern and central states, it is no wonder that farmers leave their plows, lawyers their desks, and blacksmiths their anvils. I have heard of villages divested of the male members of the population, leaving the women to attend to field and hearthstone.

"Gold! Gold! Gold!" is the cry, and if one is to judge by the various languages spoken on the streets of San Francisco, it was heard around the world. I truly believe that in a very short time San Francisco will become the most cosmopolitan of this nation's cities.

San Francisco, California
Saturday, September 21, 1850

Dear Cousin Sallie,

We have had no further word from my mother even though September is more than halfway through. I hope she is not ill.

Nearly every day I ask if we have had a new letter from her, and each time Aunt says that Uncle will surely tell me when such a letter is received at the post office. I have often wondered about my mother. Do I, perhaps, resemble her? Do I have brothers or sisters some where in this world? Do I have a father? Now, because she is alive and living in California, I am to meet my mother!

Aunt and I have found ourselves selling pies! Even though we have the cook stove, we have learned to do much of our cooking and baking out of doors, as our corrugated castle becomes very warm when the stove is in use. This was some thing we had not considered. Also, and to our regret, we have learned that even when we are not cooking or baking, with the sun beating on our roof, it can be extremely warm within. Uncle says it is only to be expected as the entire house is made of metal. Aunt and I say that may be so, but giving the reason does not make it cooler!

Like many others here, we have found that an iron kettle of good size does nicely when used over an open fire. With its lid firmly in place it serves as an oven; uncovered it makes a fine stew pot. For lesser quantities we use utensils we brought with us. They have become quite blackened for being treated in this way!

One day, as Aunt was setting our newly baked pies out to cool, a miner came along. You can always tell a miner because he will be wearing a red flannel shirt and trousers tucked into his boots. Also he will have a beard because they do not shave in the diggings.

This miner stopped when he saw Aunt. "Please, ma'am," he queried, "and might you sell me one of your pies? Since I came to this place I haven't had a bite to eat that was made by a lady."

Aunt said she was surely sorry but the pies, having been made for her family, were not for sale.

"Ma'am," said he, "your family is fortunate indeed. But supposing you agreed to sell me *two* pies and I was to pay you enough that you could buy the makings for a good many more?"

"Indeed," she said, "but I wonder if you know that eggs are costing a dollar a piece, potatoes about the same. As for the other ingredients, wheat is not grown in this region as yet, so flour is dear, and salt, like sugar, must be imported from elsewhere. About the only item we get from California is the beef!"

"Well," said he, "I can see that purchasing all those things you are talking about comes to a good bit of money. But those pies are looking so awfully good, I would give five dollars for each one, and I have the dust to do it."

When they say "dust" here, they mean gold dust, and it is used as money. The merchants have special scales and they know how much each ounce is worth, which can change. So if someone buys some thing, and wants to use dust to pay for it, they weigh it out in the correct amount.

Five dollars for each pie was indeed a good

price and Aunt quickly determined that even if we sold two to the miner, we would still have enough pies for our needs. Aunt agreed to make the sale and, he being a pleasant fellow, she engaged him in talk while I was sent to fetch Uncle's scale and some newsprint with which to wrap the pies. Uncle had purchased the scale thinking that dust would be used to pay his scholars' tuition. But establishing a school such as he has in mind has proved a much harder task than he anticipated and as yet he has neither school nor scholars. Meanwhile, Aunt and I are putting the scale to use.

Aunt and the miner were talking like old friends by the time I returned. And he did have plenty of dust! The only thing was, he ate the first of the pies right off. So we had only one to wrap. He asked us to do it up carefully so he could read the paper after he ate the pie. It did not matter that it was long out of date. He supposed the world had gone on its merry way whether he'd read of it or not. But, he said, he was interested to see where it had got to. Then he bid us good-bye and assured us that he would be certain to return on another day.

The next time our miner came, some of his

friends came too. That day's baking—with nine pies sold!—brought us forty-five dollars and Uncle said such a successful business deserved better accommodations!

On the spot he emptied two barrels of the house wares that had been packed in them, placed the barrels in front of the house with perhaps the space of three feet between them, and laid some planks across. I thought Aunt would object to his emptying of the barrels but she just busied herself in finding new places for their abruptly evicted contents—and hummed to herself as she did so.

By the time evening fell, Aunt had decided that her table deserved a covering. So the next time we had pies to sell she spread a length of cloth over the planking. We were all quite pleased with ourselves but, I said, there was one more thing needed.

I must tell you that it did not take long to find a piece of wood the right size for a sign and a bit of charcoal from last night's cook fire. I wrote FRESH PIES FOR SALE on my sign, but I did not include the price in case we decide to change it.

Now Aunt and I bake and sell pies every other day. Aunt says that is as much as she can do and besides, it is not only the cost of the fillings, it is not always easy to locate the items she needs. In between the baking and selling days I do the lessons Uncle sets for me.

Uncle has not yet been able to find a proper location for his school. He is quite particular about this but houses are being built one right after the other and it seems he has no sooner settled on a location than it has been purchased by another person. Also, the price of lumber and the cost of construction is more than he calculated. It is quite a conundrum. He cannot promise a school unless he has built it, and he cannot build it unless he has scholars who will pay. In the meantime he is working in the office of one of San Francisco's many lawyers. Why, you may wonder, are they so numerous? The answer is that with ownership of claims, etc., being hard to establish, and charges of arson and vandalism not infrequent, California is a very disputatious place.

I think a letter from you has been lost at sea. In your past letter you tell of Alice Wentworth's marriage as if I was familiar with all its circumstances. But this is the first I have heard of it.

The same is true with Tommy Fielding and how severely he was thrashed by his father for not telling the truth concerning some small matter. It is surely not the first time that Tommy has been less than honest, and not the first time he has been thrashed, either. But it is well known that Mr. Fielding is a man of bad temper, and Tommy seems ever to put himself in the line of its fire.

You say that he—Tommy—has spoken of California as a place of opportunity and has asked you how I have fared.

My situation is very different from what his might be. But it is true that many persons have come because of difficulties in their present lives as much as for the gold they expect to find. Some succeed, others are disappointed. But if the day is to come that Tommy is determined to leave New Bedford, tell him that he ought to make the voyage employed as a cabin boy. In that way he would not have to pay for his passage and he would probably enjoy better treatment than as a common sailor. I, for one, would welcome him to these shores! If his father were to regret that his son was no longer with him, he would have only himself to blame.

I hope this letter reaches you safely and that the mail ship bringing your reply does not come to grief! They say that one ship in six does not reach its destination.

With greatest affection,
Eldora

San Francisco, California
Wednesday, October 9, 1850

Dear Cousin Sallie,

My mother visited yesterday! She is taller than Aunt, and wore a taffeta dress with wide sleeves and a hoop skirt. Her hair, which is very much the same color as mine, was gathered into a chignon and held in a net of black silk. I think Aunt, wearing her brown silk with its lace collar, felt rather plainly dressed by comparison. She carried herself well, however. Uncle, as always, cut a fine figure.

My mother came in midmorning and stayed for quite some time. She and Aunt exchanged such parts of my story as were known to each. One of the first things Aunt asked about was my mother's illness. My mother replied that she had contracted cholera when we crossed overland from Chagres to Panama City. Her plan had been to continue, by boat, from Panama City to Yerba Buena, as San Francisco was then called. My father was to meet us there. However, her illness, which had worsened during the time we were in Panama City, rendered this plan unlikely. Indeed, her eventual recovery had to have been a matter of luck for no treatment was available. As for me, I had remained in good health.

We were staying in a small hotel. One morning, quite unexpectedly, the captain knocked at the door of my mother's room. He needed to tell her that his ship was to sail the next day and, because cholera was so greatly feared and the health of the other passengers had to be considered, my mother could not be taken aboard. The captain's distress was evident, my mother told us, and he had acknowledged that he could not recall when he had been required to deliver such a painful message.

"But what shall I do?" my mother had asked. "What will become of the child?"

"I do not know," was the captain's reply. "But, to the extent possible, I will help you to achieve whatever it is you decide."

The next morning he called again. My mother told him that, during a long and sad night, she had reached the difficult conclusion that she had no choice but to ask the captain to take me to my father.

Although he had grave misgivings, circumstance offered no better solution. The captain regretted that he could not linger as preparation for sailing was already under way.

There was a catch in my mother's voice as she told us how intently she had watched me until, too soon, the captain signaled that he must take his leave. My mother then rose to give him a packet of my clothes that she had prepared, kissed me once, and placed me in his arms.

Just before the captain closed the door behind us, my mother called after him. There was one more favor she must ask, she said, holding out a single earring made of amethyst and gold. Should my father require proof that I was indeed his daughter, the earring would be sufficient. The captain nodded, wrapped the earring in a handkerchief, and placed it carefully in a pocket of his coat. Then he returned my mother's attempt at a smile and left the room. He had closed the door gently. She remembered that.

As we know, the captain was unable to find my

father and there was no one with whom he could leave a small and frightened little girl. He therefore took me with him on the long voyage back to New England. Soon after returning to his home port, he prevailed on his aunt and her husband to take me into their home. He was careful to give the earring to his aunt—for safekeeping—and before he set me on her lap, he offered a single piece of advice: "She is very fond of bananas."

"I remember that well," Aunt recalled. "And I did wonder how the dear man supposed I would find bananas in New Bedford!"

When I was small, I used to beg Aunt to show me the earring and to tell the words with which my mother had instructed the captain, and which he had repeated to Aunt.

Now my mother spoke them again. Without quite knowing what I was doing, I joined her recital. "When my husband meets you," we said, "show this earring to him. It is one of the pair that was his wedding gift to me. On seeing it, he will know that I have loved him even beyond the grave and that Eldora is our child."

For the next few minutes, no one spoke—neither

Aunt, nor Uncle, nor my mother—nor I. When Aunt broke the silence, it was to ask had not Mrs. Ramos, on recovering her health, gone to Yerba Buena? And if her husband and child were not there as expected, surely she had tried to find Captain Shipman and to learn her daughter's whereabouts?

"Yes," my mother told her, "quite so. On reaching Yerba Buena many weeks later, and finding myself bereft of husband as well as child, I wrote immediately to the captain. In time my letter was returned to me, unopened. Enclosing it was a formal reply from the shipping company. Captain Shipman was no longer in their employ, they wrote. They were therefore returning my letter and 'regretted that they could be of no assistance.'"

Aunt nodded to Uncle, who then took up the story. "Perhaps we can enlighten you," he said. "Shortly after bringing Eldora to us, my wife's nephew declared himself weary of the seagoing life. The clipper ships that were his heart's delight were being pressed to make ever faster voyages and he had no taste for ships driven wholly or in part by steam. On resigning his command, my wife's nephew took up the law—a profession he has pursued successfully ever since. I should also tell you that he had become fond of Eldora and was a not-infrequent visitor to our home in New Bedford."

"I have often wondered what became of him," my mother said quietly. "It is a comfort to know that part of the story."

We none of us knew what to say, for it seemed that every thing possible had been told. But no. In another moment my mother opened her silken pocket and extracted a small object. Even before she showed it, I knew it to be the earring she had kept. And even as my mother extended her hand, Aunt mirrored the gesture. So it was that the earrings—the gold and amethyst earrings, the earrings that had been a wedding gift—were together once again.

A brief discussion followed: Should the earrings be kept as a pair, and if so, who would keep them? In the end my mother prevailed. "One day they will be Eldora's," she said. "And until the time has come . . ." She did not complete her thought but placed the second earring in Aunt's hand, and Aunt closed her fingers over the pair.

Once this moment had been reached, my mother bade us farewell and said we would surely see one another again—a sentiment echoed by Uncle, Aunt, and me. Then she signaled to her driver that she was ready to depart.

Despite the billowing of her skirt, my mother stepped gracefully into the carriage, turned to wave to us briefly, and closed the door behind her.

I stood stock-still, looking after the carriage that was taking my mother away. For just that single moment I had the thought that, had my mother meant to take me with her, I might be sitting beside her and Aunt and Uncle, sad to say good-bye, would be waving and waving to me. Instead, the three of us waved in my mother's direction until her carriage disappeared from sight and with it, my slight, sad wish.

An odd ordinariness passed over us then. The next morning, which is to say today, Aunt and I baked our pies, and in the afternoon the miners came and the sales were brisk. When the last of them had left, I told Aunt that I wished to write to you about my mother's visit. She seemed not at all surprised and certainly did not remonstrate against my doing so. If you wish, you may tell your family about this turn of affairs, but at present I have no intention of writing to others.

I must ask you to forgive the uncommon length of this letter. I have written, as closely as I am able, the exact words that were spoken.

Your loving cousin,
Eldora

SAN FRANCISCO:
FOOD, CLOTHING AND SHELTER
BY JOHN HALL

My time here has been enjoyable as well as rewarding and I can happily report on excellent meals prepared by French and German chefs. Also true is that the exotic fragrance of foods originating in the Orient and the Sandwich Islands has lured me into more exotic restaurants serving excellent food of rare and delicate flavors. As they are both generous and inexpensive, meals offered by Chinese establishments are especially popular. All of which is not to discount that one finds here elegant outposts of New York City's Delmonico's Restaurant and Chicago's Palmer House!

When I had cause to inquire about having my shirts laundered, I was directed to the area inhabited by the Chinese, many of whom do expert laundering. My informant told me that not many years ago, when the Chinese had not yet arrived on these shores in any great number, shirts *et cetera* in need of laundering were sent to mainland China. This required a voyage lasting several months. Once arrived in China, the clothes were laundered, packaged, and placed on ships bound for California where, after the long return voyage, they were duly delivered to their owners.

After I had been here some weeks, I became aware that although there is no disputing the lure of gold, it appears that the greatest profits are enjoyed by those who provide needed services to the miners or engage in provisioning them. This is because no matter how much a new arrival brings, there are always additional items to be acquired. Food that can be back-packed to the mines sells well, as do ingredients such as flour priced by the bushel, honey, potatoes, and eggs, both of the latter offered at $1 a piece.

Favored residential locations are those overlooking the bay, and this despite the fact that the hills are steep and the climb long. As San Francisco's streets are not yet paved, there are a great many mud-splashed skirts in rainy weather and a great deal of dust when it is dry. In the residential neighborhoods one still finds canvas tents and improvised cabins. But there is an increasing proportion of substantial homes of brick and wood. These last, while expensive, are the preferred materials.

Houses assembled from kits are not uncommon. Those imported from the Orient offer the convenience of precut wooden pieces; those shipped from England and the industrial north of our own country provide equivalent elements of corrugated iron. As fires are all too common here, the fact that iron houses are regarded as proof against fire recommends them to many. However, on California's many sunny days, they tend to be hot within. Presumably this is less of a problem in the colder and darker climes where they originate. I have heard horrendous stories of persons trapped inside their iron homes by doors melted to the door frames when fires raged nearby.

The onrush of new arrivals has led to some ingenuity in the matter of housing. It is not uncommon for those persons to engage space aboard the very ships on which they arrived. They then use the shipboard accommodations until they discover vacant hotel rooms, set up their kit houses (which a provident few will have shipped to coincide with their own arrival), or depart for the mines.

As crews are often decimated by the decision of sailors to join the rush for gold, many ships are stranded in port. Thus their use as floating hotels is fiscally gratifying to the shipping companies and much appreciated by those in search of lodging.

San Francisco, California
Thursday, October 24, 1850

Dear Cousin Sallie,

I have come to realize that when I last wrote to you I did not tell how my mother—for there is no longer any doubt that it was she—learned of my whereabouts in California. How foolish I feel not to have provided that information at once.

The truth is both astonishing and simple. The man who helped Uncle assemble our iron house (we did not yet call it the corrugated castle) subsequently made his way south. For several weeks he worked at one of the ranches belonging to my mother. One day she was called to that ranch to attend to some new and vexing matters.

On the second day she was there, she could not help but notice that one of the workers, newly employed, was frankly and openly staring at her. She considered it prudent to pay him no mind and followed that course as best she could.

On the third day, he spoke to her. Begging your pardon, he had said, he could not help taking note of the resemblance between herself and "a real pretty young lady" living in San Francisco.

It was unusual, he had said, to see someone that age so pretty. She had an unusual name, too: Eldora. He went on to tell how he had helped assemble an iron house for a Mr. Holt, who had had it shipped all the way from New York City! Meanwhile, he, his wife, and the girl—but my mother was no longer listening. She and my father had chosen my name, and she had never heard it used by another.

When she was able to bring her attention back to the man in front of her, it was to interrupt the rest of the story and to ask if he would repeat the name of the man for whom he had done this work. He did so, and she thanked him.

After thinking it over for several days—at first telling herself that the girl he had seen could not be the child she had put to the sea captain in Panama City, then telling herself that stranger things had happened—she knew that she would have to find out where the truth of the matter lay. So that is when she wrote the letter, the nature and consequence of which I have already described.

There are times when I think my mother's visit happened only in my dreams or imagination. The second earring lies securely and out of sight with the first, and no visible trace of her visit remains, nor is it remarked upon—either by question or comment—by Uncle or Aunt. Once, when I recalled the dark green velvet of my mother's dress, Aunt's reply made it clear that she regarded my interest as frivolous and inappropriate (words she is fond of using) and that she had no intention of discussing my mother or the color of her clothes. This surprised me. I thought she and my mother had gotten on well.

The weather has changed lately with less fog and more wind, and there have been many fires. Most of them were small and quickly extinguished. However, three days since, high winds caused a much larger fire which destroyed many homes in the poorer section of the city and also shops in the adjoining neighborhood. We are told that the streets where the fire burned are piled high with charred wood, household remnants, and articles so damaged that they cannot possibly be sold—a double loss for the merchants who own their own shops.

Remembering Uncle's description of the area in which many *Mexicanos* reside, I worried that the fire might have burned the house where Lucia and her family live. So this morning I was particularly happy when she—and her brother—appeared at our door. The clothes Miguel wore smelled of smoke, and he looked extremely tired. I surmised that he had been helping to clear away the rubble left by the fire, and was glad when he assured me that their own home had escaped the flames.

It then appeared that Miguel had come to ask if I would teach him to speak English in "good ways." He said he had been well paid for the work he had done, and now he had money with which to pay me. I said I would teach him but I thought I would not be allowed to accept money.

As you can imagine, it was not easy to explain this in two languages with not many words between us in either one of them! Indeed, just when I thought we altogether understood one another about the money, Miguel smiled and said he meant me to know that he would pay me "real money," not dust!

"No," I said. "It is not right, not good."

I think this hurt Miguel's feelings, but whether it was because of what I had said or that he did not understand, I could not tell. Then I remembered what I have heard Uncle say when someone for whom he has done a favor wishes to pay *him*. "Next time," Uncle says, "you may be the one to help me." So that is what I said to Miguel. He thought a minute, and then, having understood, he smiled. Miguel has a beautiful smile, as does Lucia.

Before they left, I told him that I would prepare a lesson for him and we would do it the next time he came.

"*Gracias*," he said to me, and to Lucia, "*Vamos*." She sulked but took his hand. I watched as they walked together down the hill.

I hope I will be able to prepare the lesson I promised, but maybe I will ask Uncle to help me.

I think of you all the time.

Eldora

We had run short of potatoes for our pies, so Aunt sent me to purchase some while she pared and diced the other vegetables. While I was gone, Luke came with a message from his father. Aunt said he seemed disappointed that I was not there.

He had come to tell us that he and his father will leave for Stockton tomorrow! Just this morning Mr. Hall learned of good accommodations on an excellent ship. He being in the midst of hurried preparations for the journey, it fell to Luke to offer his father's sincere regards and also, on his father's behalf, to apologize that he was unable to give this report himself.

Uncle has said that Mr. Hall is eager to commence his travels, so we were not entirely surprised by his quick decision. As for Luke, he told Aunt that he is eager to begin mining and is happy to leave. The way he said it, Aunt remarked, did not make a very gracious farewell.

San Francisco, California
Friday, November 1, 1850

Dear Cousin Sallie,

Mr. Hall and Luke are no longer in San Francisco and we miss their company. Aunt has been out of sorts all week, and Uncle does not have stories to tell when he returns from meeting with others about hopes and plans for the school. I worry lest they fall ill.

Many people have been stricken with cholera, so mine is no idle thought. They say that much illness comes from drinking water that is not pure. The divorced woman I told you about died. She suffered for some days with a severe catarrh which then worsened until the poor woman could neither eat nor drink, became feverish, and had difficulty breathing. She did not live long in that condition, and neighbors undertook to care for the children. Then, quite to every one's surprise, the father returned. People say he means to take the children to his wife's family. I hope they fare as well as I did—first with Captain Shipman and then with Uncle and Aunt. But, as it has turned out, my mother did not die and my story has a very different ending.

I think you would like to know that Lucia has begun to chatter in English and is not afraid to laugh when I reply in Spanish that is marred with error. Her brother has his own name for me. It is Eldora-Eldorado! He says it sings like a song!

Even now I see them making their way up the hill. I will set this letter aside, to be continued later.

Monday

In the few days that have passed, matters have changed so much that this will not be the letter I expected to write.

I think I have told you of the table that serves as our kitchen table, dining table, and work table. On Sunday mornings, that is where the three of us gather in preference to attending a regular church service. (There are several churches nearby but Aunt and Uncle do not like any of them.) Once settled at our table, we recite a thankful prayer and then Uncle will read aloud from the Bible or find an "elevating selection" from some favored book. It might be Mr. Longfellow's "A Psalm of Life," of which Uncle is very fond, or some pages from "Civil Disobedience," whose author, Mr. Thoreau, had been some thing of a friend when he and Uncle were young. This Sunday, Uncle read several of Milton's poems that Aunt particularly likes. I had the thought he did this to please her especially and was surprised that when he had completed his reading, he did not release us from our usual places around the table. Instead, he turned to Aunt and said rather mysteriously, "Lucy, our week is up."

Aunt, looking frightened, looked at him. "Edward," she said, "Ed, I cannot do it."

Uncle then got up, fetched a letter from its hiding place, and gave it to me, saying, "As Aunt is not able to tell you of this, perhaps you must read it yourself."

It was a letter addressed to both of them from my mother. In it she declared her feelings for me and set out the advantages that would be mine were I to exchange my home with Aunt and Uncle for hers!

Aunt and Uncle watched me as I read, their eyes never leaving my face. After a few minutes, during which none of us spoke, Uncle stood up, cleared his throat, and said, "Well, then . . ."

As for Aunt, she got up from the table and, forgetting to put on her apron, began to prepare our meal. Meanwhile, Uncle took up paper, pen, and inkwell but wrote nothing despite these preparations. I watched them both but remained seated, holding the letter in both my hands as if, were I to set it aside, it would take its message with it, and disappear.

After some minutes, Aunt approached me and placed several large potatoes and a paring knife before me. "As you have not left us yet," she said sharply, "I would appreciate your help."

Her words stung so greatly I feared that I would cry. If my expression gave any hint of my feelings, Aunt gave no notice, and I set to work. For the rest of the day we attended to our usual tasks—few, as it was Sunday.

Once, when I was quite small, Aunt scolded me in a way that was uncommonly severe. To her surprise, and mine, I responded by saying in an angry voice that if my mother were alive, my real mother, she would never, never, ever treat me so unkindly.

"Children do not choose their parents," Aunt had said in reply. "Nor is the choice of children generally up to the parents. Captain Shipman knew that our infant son had died, and Uncle and I accepted to care for you. But . . ."

I do not know what she meant to say beyond that, for she did not continue.

I wish you were here.

Eldora

San Francisco, California
Tuesday, November 12, 1850

Dear Cousin Sallie,

Yesterday, for no reason I could discover, Aunt located the case in which the earrings are kept. "I suppose you will want to take these with you," she said. When I did not answer, she added rather sharply, "They are yours, you know."

"But Aunt," I protested, "we have not yet decided!"

"*We* have not decided?" she repeated, changing my words into a scornful question. "*We* have not decided? It is your choice, Eldora, *your* choice. I thought we had made that clear."

"But Aunt," I said again, and when I did not continue, she looked at me with raised eyebrows, shrugged, and without saying any thing, returned the case to its hiding place.

Ever since my mother's letter was given to me to read, shrugs and gestures have taken the place of words. There is a distance between us, and I am made to feel as if the corrugated castle—which once was *ours*—is now hers and Uncle's.

The only pleasant occurrence has been a visit from Lucia and her brother. When they came yesterday, they brought a gift from their mother, their *madre*, which Miguel presented to Aunt. It was a cake, sent because I am now teaching Miguel as well as Lucia. Aunt, of course, said it was not necessary, it was too large a gift, it was my pleasure to be their teacher, and we could not accept it.

Miguel heard her out and then, half laughing said, "Sí, but now Eldora is teaching me also to write and to read! And with me it is not easy to teach."

Aunt seemed not to notice that he was joking. "Of course," she said, "you do understand, Miguel, that Eldora may not be with us much longer."

Perhaps he did not understand her, as his reply was quite cheerfully given. "Maybe," he said, "we begin *mañana*?"

"Tomorrow," I corrected.

Uncle, who had been listening, now looked up from his writing. For the first time in several days I saw him smile.

That was yesterday. Today, when Miguel arrived, I suggested that if he would write a letter in English, it would be a good way to learn.

"But," he reminded me, "in English I do not know any person—*una persona*—to write!"

I had to laugh at my own foolishness and then I said I thought he could write to you! It took a long time, more than you might think. Then Miguel was not pleased with the appearance of his first attempt. So what you see here is a fair copy. I hope that the next time you write to me you will reply to him. He would like that so much.

Have I told you that the reason Miguel cannot attend the schools here is that he is Mexican, and Mexicans, Indians, and Negroes may not attend? When I asked Uncle if he might allow Miguel to attend *his* school, Uncle said it was not possible because some of the paying students would then be withdrawn. This surprised me and troubles him. But, he said, as he came here to be a teacher, he will teach those that he can teach.

"Well," I said, "it is not against any law for me to teach Lucia and Miguel. And I am glad to have Mexican students!"

"I am glad for them," Uncle said, "and proud of you."

It has made me quite cheerful to write to you and especially to tell you about Lucia and Miguel and what Uncle said to me. Perhaps, if Aunt will have me, I can stay here, and teach Lucia and Miguel, and visit my mother from time to time and she will visit me!

I think I would like that. But I am plagued by the thought that Aunt has been kind to me only because it was believed that I was an orphan and there was no place for me to go. But now that we know my mother did not die and is here in California . . .

It is all very confusing and just as a dog will chase his tail, so one thought chases another.

I hope you are well and I will write to you when I know if I am to stay here or go to San Pedro, where my mother lives.

Eldora

TO SALLIE FROM MIGUEL

November 12, 1850

Dear Miss Cousin Sallie,

This is my first letter in English. Your cousin is helping me. She is very kind and nice.

There are many *Americanos* here. They want to find gold.

I think that is not a good thing. When they find gold they spend it in bad ways. If I would find gold I would give it to my mother. Then she can build a house. We have a big family and a small house. That is why she must build a new house. My father is not here or he would build a house.

Your friend,
Miguel

San Francisco, California
Monday, November 18, 1850

Dear Mother,

How long I have envied those who have often and easily written those two small words. Now they are mine to write.

Dear Mother, yes.

I wish to make San Pedro my home and to live with you at your inn. I have thought about it long and hard. The next time you come to San Francisco, I will be ready to go to San Pedro with you. Please tell us when you expect to arrive.

I believe that Aunt and Uncle had hoped I would make a different choice, as they have had little to say since I told them what I intend. Aunt has promised to wash and mend my clothes as may be necessary and Uncle has wished me well more than once.

I think that is all I have to say just now. Please write to tell me when you will come.

Your daughter,
Eldora

CHAPTER II

NOVEMBER 12, 1850 – FEBRUARY 28, 1851

Your friend I hope,
LUKE

LUKE TO ELDORA,
LETTER OF NOVEMBER 23, 1850

Roaring Springs, California
November 12, 1850

Dear Eldora,

When Pa sent me to tell Mr. and Mrs. Holt that he would be leaving San Francisco the next day and me with him, I thought it would give me a chance to say good-bye to you. Also, I meant to ask if it would be all right with you if I were to write to you when I was traveling with Pa, and if you thought Mr. and Mrs. Holt would mind.

So I had a lot of questions to ask and was disappointed that you, having been sent to buy potatoes, were not at home. So after I gave Mrs. Holt the message from Pa, I asked her about me writing to you. She said she saw no reason why I should not do that. But, she said, she had no idea as to whether or not you would reply. Well, I was not even thinking about you answering! I just wanted to know about me writing to you.

I meant to write a lot sooner than now, but when Pa and I were in Stockton, there was not much to say. Stockton is not as big as San Francisco, but many men pass through both cities on their way to the diggings. Because of that they are the same in many ways, and in both cities there are saloons and restaurants and stores where supplies are sold. One difference is that in San Francisco they worry about fires but in Stockton they worry about floods.

The day before Pa and I were to leave Stockton, I told him I had been thinking about the way he had things planned out and that I did not wish to travel all the way to Sacramento before we ever got to the mines. I told him I had heard men say they had got two or three hundred dollars a day mining, and I was eager to try my hand at it.

So then Pa asked what I meant to do with so much money. Well, I said, I thought I would know what to do with the money once I had it. Pa thought I was sassing him, which ended the conversation.

By the next day Pa had gotten over being angry and was purely sorry about me not traveling with him. I said I was sorry too about not traveling with him, and he said he thought we might go to the diggings first. That was good news to me! Maybe, he said, I could stay there for some weeks or even longer and he would go on the way he'd planned.

We traveled quite companionably after that and I was even sorry to think we would soon be saying good-bye to one another, but not sorry enough to change my mind.

We had been directed to a place called Roaring Springs, and we reached it after traveling two days. It is in the diggings (which they pronounce "diggins") and is said to be a very likely place. That is where I am now.

We heard of other camps where they started mining and then quit because there wasn't any gold in the first place or it was already mined. I am fixing to get $1,000 once I start mining. Pa says I will be lucky to get half that much.

We have got it arranged the way Pa said. I will stay here while he continues his travels. While I am here, I will stay with a miner by the name of Charley Higgins. I could not help but think that it is an exact rhyme for "diggins," but of course I did not say so. I am supposed to help Charley however he asks and he will teach me about mining. Pa says that if mining is what I want to do, this is a good way to learn about it.

Mr. Higgins says it is all right for me to call him Charley when it is just the two of us. Otherwise I should address him more respectfully. It looks like I am the youngest one here. Several of the men have got their wives with them. There are no children or even babies.

Every one is telling me that mining is nothing but hard work. Well, I know that. But they have to be finding some gold here or else they would not stay.

Charley has been a miner since they discovered gold. In fact, he was there when the first gold was found in a millrace they were building. Charley said that some will tell you that Mr. Sutter, who owned the mill and a lot of land around it, tested those first bits of gold himself and that he used aqua fortis, a strong chemical, from his own apothecary. But there are others who say it had to do with the weight of the flakes they found compared with the weight of coins they knew to be gold. Mr. Higgins says there are a lot of such stories. But he was there when it happened so I think the way he tells it is probably the story to believe.

First, Charley says, you have to know that there was a camp cook and laundress there, and she was named Jennie Wimmer. She was the mother of some seven children, and wife to a miner named Peter Wimmer. But the story is about her, not the children and not him.

Jennie was making soap one morning and along about midmorning she heard loud arguing and a big commotion going on. It was about what they had found and if it was gold or not. After a while she spoke up and said all they had to do was throw those flakes into her soap-making kettle and let them stay over-night. That, she said, would prove it one way or the other.

As you can imagine, the men were none too happy about throwing their gold—if indeed it was gold—into Jennie Wimmer's kettle. Then someone said that Jennie was right and that the lye would not harm gold the way it does other metals. So if those shiny little flakes and pebbles were still there in the morning, they could be sure that what they were looking at was gold. But, as Mr. Higgins said, if there was nothing left, it would not have been gold in the first place. So nothing would be lost by the experiment.

It was gold, all right. But there was a worrisome moment when Jennie Wimmer's soap, which had formed, was cut into pieces and there was nothing in any one of them. Some of the boys, as Mr. Higgins calls them, were shouting and yelling and close to getting into fisticuffs about letting a woman have her way. But Mrs. Wimmer just told them to hush up and pay attention, like she does with her four boys and three girls. Then she plunged her hands into the bottom of the kettle, and there was the gold—just little bits of it, but shining as bright as could be.

I asked Mr. Higgins if the potash wouldn't hurt her hands, and he said that after all she'd been through it would take more than potash to hurt Jennie Wimmer's hands. I was going to ask what she had been through but he changed the subject.

I think Mr. Higgins is glad to have someone (me) to tell his stories to. Lucky for me, he tells good stories. I am pretty sure that it was Mrs. Wimmer's lye that proved that the gold was gold. But you never can tell for a certainty if a fellow should believe all that is told him here.

Pa has been gone three days now. I miss him, but in all other ways I am fine and hoping you are the same.

From,
Luke Hall

Roaring Springs, California
November 16, 1850

Dear Mother,

I am not in Stockton with Pa or in any of the other places he means to visit before returning to San Francisco. Roaring Springs is a mining camp, and that is where I am. I mean to stay here six or seven weeks. We came directly from Stockton, and Pa stayed just long enough to see to it that I will be all right. After he has finished the rest of his travels, he will return to Roaring Springs and we will go back to San Francisco together.

Pa said he was going to write to you about what he calls "the details" of how we have got things arranged. But, he said, I ought to write my own letter telling you how it is to be here, which I said I meant to do anyway. He said he was glad to hear that. Then he reminded me that you were not too pleased about me making this trip in the first place. So, he said, I should not fill up my letter with worrisome things.

Roaring Springs is a mining camp and it is said to be a likely place to try my luck at mining. I am to stay with a miner by the name of Charley Higgins while I am here. Pa says that if mining is what I want to do, this is a good way to learn about it. Mr. Higgins has been a miner since gold was first discovered and in fact he was employed by Mr. Sutter when that event occurred.

Mr. Higgins is older than Pa but more spry. He had a partner here, but they got in a fight and the partner left soon thereafter. Mr. Higgins says if I just mind my business, which his first partner did not do, I will not have that kind of trouble or any other kind either. One good thing that is left over from when the partner was here is the cabin they built. Mr. Higgins is especially pleased with the glass windows they put in, and Pa was happy to see that the cabin is well situated and big enough for two people. It is a lot more comfortable than a tent. Two men who have got their wives here also have cabins but mostly the miners live in tents.

Some of the men have gotten $200 or $300 in one

day of mining. I told Mr. Higgins I'd heard about a woman who was sweeping the dirt floor of her cabin and turned up more than $500. Mr. Higgins said that when it comes to mining, people will tell many stories, but most of them are not true. Personally he did not think that gold in a cabin floor was one of the true ones.

I am the youngest one here and every one is telling me that mining is hard work at any time of year, and in the winter the snow can get so deep that the camps are snowed in. The hard work does not worry me any and I will not be here when it is winter.

Up till now I have only panned for gold with Mr. Higgins. Yesterday he said it was time for me to try it by myself. When we weighed what panned out for me, all I got was $2.56. Charley—that is Mr. Higgins—said that some days are like that and I should not be discouraged. But it is a long way to the $1,000 that I told Pa I meant to get.

I am saving the cap and mittens you knitted for me for when it is really cold. So far it is not. How is Millfield these days? Have others left to go mining, or is Pa—who is not interested in mining for gold— the only one to head out to California?

II. LUKE

I hope this letter finds you well. So far I am doing fine so I hope it does not worry you to think of me being here without Pa.

Your son,
Luke

Later.

I do not know when I will be able to post this letter but I will do it as soon as I can or give it to someone and ask them to post it.

Roaring Springs, California
November 23, 1850

Dear Eldora,

I know you do a lot of letter-writing to your cousin
and maybe some others that I do not know about.
But what will you say when I tell you that I am
writing letters that are not my own, but for other
people? Plus, I am getting paid for doing it.

The way it happened is this: One of the miners
came up to me the other day and said he had seen
me sitting outside of Charley Higgins's cabin and
writing. So he was wondering if maybe I would write
some thing for him.

"What do you mean?" I queried, being surprised
at his question.

He is from Illinois and he said there was a
girl back in Illinois that he likes a lot. "She is real
pretty," he said, "with black hair that curls in the
nicest way, and every thing to go with it." He said

he hoped she'd be waiting for him when he was done mining and back to where he was from. He'd been thinking that a letter—especially if it was written out all nice and fancy and no words spelled wrong—might help her to keep him in mind. But, he said, she could read better than he could write. So if I would write the letter for him, he thought that would help a lot.

"But what am I to tell her?" I asked.

"Oh," he said, "you need not worry about that. I will tell you what I am thinking about and all you have to do is set it down on paper."

That sounded pretty interesting. It got even more interesting when he went on to say he would pay me for doing it because he did not want me to think he was just asking a favor. Well, I had a hard time to keep a plain face when he said that, and not show how surprised I was.

How much was he thinking of paying me? I asked. "Well," he said, "five dollars for the first one and if it gets me a good answer, it might go up from there." That sounded good to me.

He was purely serious about it all and gave me $5 in dust when we got done.

It seems the news got around pretty quick! The next day, Charley and I quit early. We had done some panning, but all we had come up with was maybe $10 worth and that was not enough to keep at it. When we got back to the cabin, another one of the boys was waiting for me.

He had no idea when there would be mail going out, but he wanted me to write his letter right away—before he forgot what he wanted to say. I said I would do it and that the first fellow had paid me $5.

"I will do better than that," said he, "if you were to do it right now and not keep me waiting around. So what I'm saying is, I would pay you dust worth seven dollars and a half, with you choosing the scale."

As you can imagine, I said that would be fine and I went and got some paper and ink and a pen pretty quick so he would not lose his courage or change his mind. He did not.

The one thing he asked before we got started was he made me swear I would not tell any one what was in his letter. Well, a promise is a promise. So all I can tell you is that probably, when she gets to reading the letter, it will make her blush.

Charley thinks it is all very funny—me writing letters for men a whole lot older than I am. But he never asks what the boys are having me set down for them. And he keeps my money in a safe place, separate from his.

If I keep on writing letters—I have already written six—it might turn out that I make more money writing than mining. I never did care for learning penmanship. But then, I never thought "writing a fine hand" would do me that kind of good.

Your friend I hope,
Luke

In case you are wondering, this is my own letter—written by me and in my own words!

ON MINES, MINERS
AND MINING
BY JOHN HALL

Although I had made good and sincere efforts to
learn about mining beforehand, I was soon to be
reminded that it is one thing to read about a region
and another to be there. I knew, for example, that the
term "diggings"—or "diggins," as it is pronounced
here—refers to areas in which gold is being mined. I
had not, however, quite understood that two quite different processes are both described as mining: using
knives and pick-axes to wrest gold from the stony hill-
sides of the region, and washing gold from the beds of
streams and rivers.

Where the latter method is employed, miners use
pans, which are utensils shaped rather like skillets, to
scoop out silt by the panful. The laden pans are then
agitated with a swirling motion so that the common
silt is washed away but the gold, it being heavier,
remains.

The same principle applies to operations involv-
ing wooden "rockers," which are widely used. This
process may be described as an elaboration of simple

panning for gold. Likely streams in which, or near which, gold has been found, are diverted and their water is made to flow through the wooden troughs of well placed rockers. As with panning, described above, the common silt is washed away by the water that flows over it while the gold, being heavier, remains. It is no coincidence that the first gold was found in a millrace under construction.

To my easterner's eyes, the camps where the miners (and those wives who accompany them) live are more than camps but less than villages. One settlement I visited boasted a Main Street, along which several shops were located. They shared that somewhat grandiose address with several saloons, where gambling was an expected, indeed a principal, activity. There was a building proclaiming itself a hotel, and one restaurant serving both food and spiritous drinks.

I was told that the previous owner of this establishment did so brisk a business selling whiskey at $1 a glass that the next day he refilled the barrel with water and was delighted to repeat his success. I have no reason to doubt my informant, who further assured me that the rascal was able to continue his deception for two weeks. Whether or not this explains his rather abrupt leave-taking remains an open question. One thing is certain: Mining is not the only way for a man to get rich in the diggings.

Roaring Springs, California
November 30, 1850

Dear Eldora,

I guess you know already about Pa and how he broke
his ankle. Probably you knew about it before I did,
and probably you know more than I do now, as he
had to return to San Francisco and is still there.

The way Pa began his letter telling me about his
accident was by joking that maybe Ma was right to
caution an oldster such as he is about adventuring
on foot in California. But the rest of the letter was
serious, starting with how he caught his foot in a
root, fell smack down, and could not get up. He could
see that his ankle, being bent clear out of shape,
was broken, and there was no use thinking about
getting up and walking.

Pa said he was lucky not to be hurt any worse
than a broken ankle and also that the first person
to come along was polite, helpful, and kind. Since

Pa could not walk and did not have a horse, the man helped Pa onto the horse he had been riding and, with him going along on foot, the stranger led the way to the nearest camp. Pa stayed there until the next morning. By that time the ankle had swelled up even worse. So Pa borrowed two horses and found someone who would go to San Francisco with him. Pa rode part of the way, meaning as far as Stockton, and then went the rest of the way by ship.

In case you are wondering, there are some doctors in the diggings and some persons who just declare themselves doctors and seem to cure as many patients as the others. But Pa had the idea that a San Francisco doctor would be better and also Pa has friends there, especially Mr. and Mrs. Holt.

It was a long letter Pa wrote, maybe the longest one I ever had from him. I told Charley about it, and how the San Francisco doctor gave Pa opium when he set the bone. Pa never took opium before and he believes it helped more than whiskey would have done. Now he has two wooden slats, one bandaged to each side of his ankle, to keep it straight while it heals. Pa wrote that he is used to birch bark being used that way, but not wooden slats. As there are no birch trees in San Francisco, they have to use some thing else. He has crutches for when he walks.

It will probably be a couple of months before Pa can do much traveling! He is impatient already, but in the meantime he is helping Mr. Holt however he can and also writing some. He has some more dispatches in mind, which he means to send to the *Herald*, and he is thinking of writing a book. He would like to call it *Travels in the West*, even though right now he is not doing much traveling. Pa says being in San Francisco when the news about statehood arrived gave him the idea. I am not sure what that had to do with it.

In his letter Pa says that the ship that brought the news flew a banner with letters so large that its message, CALIFORNIA ADMITTED, could be read half way across the bay! I would have liked to see that. Did you see it?

Pa says he missed seeing it because, with his ankle the way it is, he has to stay in his hotel. The first he knew of California being the 31st state was guns and cannons going off. At first he did not know what that might mean and he wondered if it was good news or bad. But then he saw people running in the direction of Portsmouth Square and carrying flags of every kind and yelling hurrah and singing patriotic songs. So he knew it was good news and then someone told him for sure. But I guess you know all this because you were there.

Pa says that now that California is a state, it is no longer correct to speak of "the States" when referring to those that are on the eastern side of the country. "For better or for worse," he wrote, "California is a state as much as the rest. And let us hope that, as a free state, California will have laws that will not benefit some citizens and exclude others."

To tell the truth, I think the real reason Pa wrote about all of this was because he was having a hard time telling me that he can not come back to Roaring Springs when my six weeks are up. That is the way it is with Pa. If he has some thing difficult to say, he will put in a lot of other things first. What worries him is how I will get back to San Francisco.

Charley is just the opposite. When I told Charley about Pa being hurt, Charley said right off that he guessed he would be the one to make sure I got back safely. To tell the truth, I hope that is what happens.

Charley knows just about every thing there is

to know about this place and it could be interesting to travel with him. One thing he said surprised me, though. It was that if he was the next one to have an accident, or if any other thing should happen to him, Clarence Brown was the person to call on and he would help me. He is a miner, a good bit younger than Charley, and his cabin is the next one over. Charley says he is a kind and honest man.

The other thing Charley said was that it sounded to him like Pa might have been near to Hangtown when he fell. In that case Pa was truly fortunate that the first person to come along was inclined to be helpful. Hangtown got its name because it is a pretty quick-tempered place when it comes to bandits, thieves, and other villains. You would think that hanging so many of them would have taken care of things, mostly. But from what Charley knows about Hangtown, the next person to come along might have been more likely to empty Pa's pockets—or do some other kind of harm—than to help him.

Maybe Pa knew more about this than he exactly told me.

I see I have written an awful lot about me, Pa,

and California! Has your mother visited yet? I some
times wonder how it will be to see her after such a
long time and if she will look the way you remember
her to look—or maybe you do not remember, you
being so little when she sent you away. I hope she
is nice!

Your friend,
Luke

San Francisco, California
December 18, 1850

Dear Eldora,

I am back in good old San Francisco, which I reached
five days since. When we were about halfway back,
Charley told me, which he had not done before we
started out, that it would not have been safe for me
to travel by myself, and look what happened to Pa.
When I asked how it was that he was planning to go
back to the diggings by himself, he kind of laughed.
That, he said, was just one of the bigger differences
between us. And if I hadn't got that figured out yet,
he didn't see much use in explaining it.

As I had not had any letters, except the one from
Pa, while I was at Roaring Springs, I did not know
that you have decided to live with your mother in San
Pedro. So it was more than a surprise to discover that
you were no longer in San Francisco and that you had
left a little more than a week before I got there.

Pa is still here but I am staying with Mr. and Mrs. Holt, which might surprise you. When Charley brought me back from Roaring Springs, Pa was staying at the Imperial Hotel, where we had stayed when we first came. This time, because of his ankle, he has a room of his own—not just a curtained-off space.

Pa's room is large enough for me to stay there with him and that is what he thought I should do. But when he told Mr. and Mrs. Holt about me staying at the hotel with him, they said that they supposed he could stay there and keep his wits about him. But, they said, the Imperial Hotel was not a "suitable" place for an "impressionable" boy. Probably they are right. The hotel's first floor is mostly a saloon and gambling hall, and the fancy ladies who entertain there would make your eyes pop. So that is why I am staying with Mr. and Mrs. Holt, and Pa visits often.

I am using the space that was yours when you were here, so no need to describe it. I keep my clothes there (not many), my Bible that my ma gave me, and a small book meant for children that I found near Roaring Springs. I mean to show it to Lucia, but so far I have not seen her.

Pa and Mr. Holt get into long conversations. They

agree about most things (including politics and the Fugitive Slave Law) and about saloons, crime, and gambling (which they hold to be related).

They do not mind if I listen.

Mr. Holt lived in Meredith which is in New Hampshire, when Pa lived there! That is where he had his first job as a teacher and also where he met Mrs. Holt, except she was not Mrs. Holt then. He remembers my mother, who had been one of his students. Asa Shipman, the sea captain who brought you to New Bedford, had been one of his students too. Pa knew both of them well, and Pa and Mr. Holt both knew Captain Shipman's sister, Cassie, who died that year. Pa remembers her especially. Mrs. Holt was outside selling her pies, while all this talking was going on. But when they got to the part about Captain Shipman, Mr. Holt just jumped up from where he was sitting. "Lucy," he yelled in an excited voice, "you need to come in here right now!"

When she hurried in, wondering what had happened, Mr. Holt assured her that every thing was all right and then he told it all over again and we were just astonished, even me and Pa who had already heard it.

Charley, that's Mr. Higgins, did not stay in San Francisco after he brought me here. He said there are too many people living too close together for his liking. When I said I thought it was exciting and that was one of the reasons I liked it, he said he guessed that was just another of the differences between us.

To my mind the corrugated castle is still where you live. So at first it felt strange, me being here. I am getting used to it, though, and I am getting to like Mr. Holt and Mrs. Holt. I guess I do not have to tell you that they are strict but fair about what they expect.

It is mostly good to be here but I miss Roaring Springs. I wonder, does a person always miss the place where he is not?

Your friend,
Luke

San Francisco, California
January 12, 1851

Dear Eldora,

I have two things to tell you that I think you will like to know.

Number One, I have got a job, for pay, at a store that sells miners' supplies. You might think I do not know enough about mining to do that, but many of the customers have just got here and they know even less. Mr. Lewisohn, who owns the store, is Jewish. His whole family came to California with him and they live in a flat above the store. Several of Mr. Lewisohn's sons help out in the store and he treats me the same as them.

Number Two, Miguel and I have gotten to be friends. Maybe he is the best friend I ever had. He knows enough English to talk about a lot of things. I tell him that if he has to ask about some words or does not say them correctly, that is all right with me, as I am not a great talker but for different reasons.

Maybe that is why some people think I am stupid (the schoolmaster in Millfield) or rude (a neighbor in Millfield who was always telling my parents about me) or ill tempered (my mother).

One thing Miguel and I talk about is me and the diggings. In truth, it has given him the idea that he will go there. He said that if he found a lot of gold, he would give it to his mother so she could build a better house than the one she has now.

I thought Mr. and Mrs. Holt would like to hear this, so I told them. Instead, they became very worried for Miguel and found opportunity to speak with him about it. They reminded him that the diggings were known for what they called "endless, bitter, dangerous strife" between miners and claim jumpers—many of whom were Mexican. It was, they said, a particularly dangerous place for all persons of that race.

But I think Miguel will go anyway, probably in March. That is said to be a good time as the rain will have melted the snow, the streams will be higher, and there will be new sand and silt along the sandbars.

The first time Miguel came and you were not here, he left rather quickly. I think he was meaning to say *adiós* to you, but you had already gone to San Pedro. I was glad when he came again and that was the visit when he asked me if I would help him to learn more English. He would like to be able to read books like the ones Mr. Holt has on his shelf—not just the titles.

I can think of a lot of people—especially my old teacher in Millfield—who would laugh at the idea of my being a teacher to *anybody*! But I did not say this to Miguel. I just told him I would think about me helping him to learn English and he should come back in a few days and I would tell him the answer.

When he came back, I said I would try. I did not tell him that what helped me make up my mind was thinking that it would be interesting for me to try to be a good influence for a change.

Usually Miguel and Lucia come together. We take turns at pointing to things and saying what they are called in Spanish and then in English and then we ask each other questions, which they are supposed to answer in English and I am supposed to answer in Spanish. Some times we get mixed up about which language we are meant to speak and then we laugh about it. But the good thing is that I am learning Spanish just as much as they are learning English.

I remember one time when Mr. Holt said that it is not just students who learn; the teachers learn too. That did not seem to be the way it was when I was going to school in Millfield and I thought I had misunderstood Mr. Holt. Now I think that me learning Spanish while Lucia and Miguel learn English could be what he meant.

Lucia is still shy with me.

Yesterday was Miguel's fourth time, and we were looking at pictures in a book that Mr. Holt let me borrow. One picture showed bigger trees than any I have ever seen. Miguel said that once, with his *padre*, he saw such trees. They are a "big way" from here but one day he would like to go to see them with me.

When I told Mr. Holt about the trees he said that in English they are called redwoods. The reason they are so big, he said, is that they do not burn and, as they are not destroyed by forest fires, they just keep on growing. Mr. Holt is good at explaining things (even things he never saw) and this was pretty interesting. You probably know that is not true for every thing he will tell about, but I listen anyway because you never know how it will turn out.

When I asked Mr. Holt how he knows so much about redwoods, he said he had read about them. He wondered if I had ever thought about how books can tell you things you never even imagined. Well no, I said, I had not thought about books in that way, but maybe I should. He laughed when I said that, but in a friendly way.

Maybe you can ask your mother if she has ever seen redwood trees and if she can take you to see them. If she does, I hope you will tell me!

When I was at Roaring Springs I used to think about you. I hoped that you would have forgotten, or forgiven, that I was so unpleasant when we first met. I hoped that we could be friends when I came back to San Francisco but I did not imagine that you would not be here then.

Your friend,
Luke

San Francisco, California
January 27, 1851

Dear Eldora,

When Miguel came with Lucia today, he told me that some times they have come and I am not here. That made me realize that they did not know about me working for Mr. Lewisohn and that I would have to explain that I work at his store five days each week but not Saturday and Sunday. On Saturday, if you are Jewish, you are not allowed to work because it is their Sabbath and the store is closed. The store *is* open on Sunday, but that is our Sabbath day and Mr. Holt says I should respect it.

I tried my best but could not explain to Lucia and Miguel—either in English or Spanish—why I was there most days but not the other two. Finally I had the idea that I could *show* them what I meant instead of telling them about it.

I began by acting out what I do in the store, and then I said, *"Lunes, sí. Martes, sí. Miércoles, sí,"* and so on. But when I got to *sábado*, which is Saturday, I put my hands straight down at my sides and stood still and said, *"¡Sábado, no!"* This made Miguel burst out laughing, and Lucia, too. But I have to tell you that that was the end of my acting out the words because the next one was *"¡Domingo, no!"* and with all of us still laughing, I could not keep a serious face. I think it was the first time I heard Lucia laugh and I think that laughing like that showed that it was not just me and Miguel that were friends, but all three of us.

The next time they came, Lucia did not say anything but just started helping Mrs. Holt, who was setting out that day's pies. Mrs. Holt seemed pleased to have a helper. When it came time for Miguel and Lucia to leave, Mrs. Holt gave Lucia two pies to take home and some cloth that could be a blanket for No-Name which, as you know, is her doll. You could tell that Mrs. Holt was pleased to have a helper, even a small one. I wonder if Lucia reminds Mrs. Holt of when you were small.

I hope I will get a letter from you soon.

Your friend,
Luke

San Francisco, California
February 28, 1851

Dear Eldora,

Thank you for telling me that you have gotten my letters and that you are glad to get them. So here is some thing I think you will like to know about. It happened last week when I was teaching Lucia and Miguel. But first you have to know that when I was in the diggings I found a child's book alongside a trail, or did I tell you that when it happened? Olive is the name written inside the cover. I kept the book all the time I was at Roaring Springs so I could give it back to her if I ever met or heard about a girl named Olive, but I never did.

For no special reason, I took the book with me when I returned to San Francisco. It has many small pictures and when I started to help Lucia learn English, Lucia and I began to use Olive's book. That made me feel better about keeping it.

Just this past Monday, we were naming—in English—the objects in the pictures. Miguel was watching us, half listening and, once in a while, smiling when Lucia learned a new word.

After we looked at the pages we already knew, we came to one we had not talked about before. It showed a two-storey house with a fence around it. There were flowers growing beside the fence, and a roadway leading to the house. There were trees on either side of the roadway and a pony cart waiting in front of the house. Lucia looked at it a long time without saying any thing, and then she pronounced it, "*Un palacio.*"

I will agree that it looked like a very fine house. But it was a house, all the same. So I said, "No. Not *palacio*, Lucia. *Casa.* House." But, in a way that was most unlike her, Lucia insisted that the picture showed a *palacio*. That I had called it a house seemed to her an error.

We went over it and over it, but nothing changed her mind—or mine. My *casa* was her *palacio*, and that was all there was to it.

I had never seen Lucia insist so strongly on any thing! And when I tried to turn the page to another picture, Lucia protested. It was *un palacio*, and I was to agree before we looked at any other picture!

At first it was funny, but then it stopped being funny and I began to get cross with her. That was when Miguel leaned over and, with a pencil he had with him and a sheet of the foolscap Mr. Holt had provided for the lessons, Miguel began to draw.

As if by magic, a house appeared on the paper, a small adobe that looked so real you could almost smell the food cooking over the open fire that he had drawn in front of the house!

"So!" Lucia exclaimed triumphantly, pointing at Miguel's drawing and at the picture in the book, then identifying the one as a house and the other as a palace. Lucia, I was discovering, can be very strong minded!

By now all three of us had forgotten the house in the book, and Miguel was adding a woman with a market basket to his drawing. *"Mi casa* and *mi madre,"* Lucia said with great certainty.

We were soon to realize that Miguel did not consider the picture finished. Squinting at it, he drew another, smaller figure that Lucia, with delight, recognized as herself. Then there appeared a pig, several chickens, a cat followed by two kittens, and a goat!

Miguel went on drawing for quite some time. It was wonderful to watch him and to see the neighboring house that soon appeared on the page. It was followed by several children playing and a rider on a horse—in truth I cannot remember all that he added. Only when the page was full did Miguel put down his pencil. Then, with evident pleasure, he said, "*Todo.*"

They left soon thereafter, and I put Miguel's picture alongside Olive's book—as we have come to call it—on the big table.

Mrs. Holt was preparing our supper when Mr. Holt returned to the castle. The drawing was just about the first thing he saw, and he stopped in front of it—and just *stared*.

"Lucy," he called, "have you seen this? The work is quite remarkable, and whoever has made it is an artist!"

"The person who has made it," she said, "is Miguel. And I, too, am quite startled at how well wrought the figures are."

But Mr. Holt had more to say than that. "The boy's

skill is truly astonishing," he added. "No student of mine has ever made such a drawing. It is really quite extraordinary," he said, "and most unexpected!"

That night I fell asleep thinking that if you and Lucia had not met one another by chance, and if I had not found Olive's book or started teaching Lucia and Miguel, and if Lucia and I had not disagreed about the picture in the book, then Miguel would never have made his drawing, and then none of this would have come to pass, for it is all connected!

I hope you are finding new friends in San Pedro— and also that you have not altogether forgotten your old friend, Luke.

Two days later

Miguel has made up his mind about going to the diggings. He hopes to go to Roaring Springs, as that is the camp I told him about. He said he wished to tell you about this himself. I helped him write the letter, which I am sending with this one and which he wrote.

Luke

Friday, February 28, 1851

Dear Eldora-Eldorado,

I have written your name that sings like a song because that is how it sings in my mind.

Your friend Luke says that when I am finished writing this letter he will send it. I hope it is all right for me to write to you. I am going to go to the diggings soon so do not be surprised if I am not here when you come to visit. I hope I will find a lot of gold and I will give it to my mother. I hope your mother is not mad for you to have a letter from a friend who is *Mexicano*. Maybe you do not tell her!

I am glad for you that your true mother found you after so long a time. But I am sorry it has taken you away from this place.

I am glad Luke is teaching me and Lucia, too. He is a good teacher. He says he is learning too.

Some times Luke shows me newspapers that Mr. Holt has bought. He teaches me words to read.

Luke says his father is a newspaper writer. I think it would be good to be a newspaper writer and tell the truth to people.

I hope you are happy to live with your mother. But all here miss you very much. It will be good if you will visit some day.

From your friend,
Miguel

CHAPTER III

Eldora

DECEMBER 19, 1850 – MAY 7, 1851

*I am beginning to realize just how
lonely a princess can be.*

ELDORA TO COUSIN SALLIE
LETTER OF MARCH 15, 1851

San Pedro, Salinas Valley, California
Thursday, December 19, 1850

Dear Cousin Sallie,

I have been here a week! The journey from San Francisco took the better part of four days. It covered about 130 miles. Up to this moment my thoughts have been so jumbled I could not set them down, not even to you. But now, starting on the day I left San Francisco, I will try.

My mother had said that an early departure would be to our advantage. At the appointed hour Aunt, Uncle, and I stood at the door of the corrugated castle, awaiting my mother's carriage. With Aunt's help I had packed my belongings the night before. The hardest part was when she gave me the earrings and said that now they must be mine.

It was evident that the carriage had been freshly washed for the return journey, and the horses were in high spirits. We all greeted one another and then, not knowing what to say, fell silent, and Uncle carried my trunk from the house and set it down next to the carriage. Alberto, who has a wooden leg and is my mother's driver, asked, "¿*Todo?*" meaning, "Is that all?"

I was ashamed to have so few things of my own. Uncle seemed not to notice.

We did not linger over our good-byes, which were difficult. My mother indicated that I was to enter the carriage ahead of her, which I did, seating myself close to the nearest window. I had not realized how high up it was, and was therefore surprised at how small Aunt and Uncle looked, and the corrugated castle also. At a command from Alberto the horses started up, and we moved away quickly. Aunt's white handkerchief, waving good-bye, was the last thing I could see. When I could not see it any more, I cried. It was the first, but not the only, time that day.

I tried to wipe the tears away with the back of my hand, but my mother saw me and gave me a hand-kerchief to use. As soon as I gave it back to her, the handkerchief vanished. My mother saw my surprise.

"Trick," she said with a little smile. I must have looked puzzled when she said this for she leaned closer and showed me how she had tucked the handkerchief under the cuff of her sleeve. I was glad that she did not talk about my crying, because I was ashamed. After a while I fell asleep.

It was high noon when we stopped at a ranch (*ranchos*, they are called here). We had our dinner there and also changed horses. When we returned to the carriage, I again fell asleep. By the time I woke up the sun had shifted to the west. The road had become quite steep and deeply rutted. The carriage was tilting this way and that. I think it was the tilting that woke me up. I stayed awake after that, just looking out at the land we were passing and speaking only when my mother asked me a question.

Later, when we stopped to change horses again, several *rancheros*, who could be mistaken for miners except that they are differently dressed, were standing around. They asked if we were hungry and, when my mother said we surely were, they offered a good but simple meal. Watching the preparations, I wondered if Aunt would continue to make and sell pies now that I am gone and if any one will help her.

Just before sunset we found ourselves in a valley. I watched the clouds over the hills turn orange and then pink. The sun set soon afterward and we stopped at a small inn where the proprietor knew my mother and welcomed her. He would be happy if we would stay the night. "*Mi casa es su casa*," he said, meaning "My house is your house." It would, he said, be an honor.

Even as he spoke I saw my mother eyeing the two large tables in the public room.

"Yes," the proprietor acknowledged, "one is for dining and the other for gaming." I could see that my mother was not made happy by this, and guessed that she had not anticipated how it would be to travel with a daughter—me!

However, there was no other hotel nearby and the horses were weary. Having no choice in the matter, my mother accepted the innkeeper's offer of a beautiful room—the most beautiful in the hotel!—and the meal was excellent. I believe that Alberto ate with those who had prepared the meal. He did not eat with us.

The second day of our journey passed in much the same way as the first. We stayed the second night at a *rancho* where again the owner welcomed my mother warmly. That was when I began to realize that my mother knows, and is known by, a great many people in this part of the state.

On the third day of our journey the sun was at its highest when my mother called to Alberto and instructed him to stop. She then pointed to an east-running road that crossed the one on which we were traveling.

"If we were to take that road," my mother said, "and follow it for one day, maybe two, it would bring us to the mountains. There is land there that belonged to my husband." He had purchased it, she said, for no other reason than that he found the mountains beautiful. Often he would go there by himself, and when he returned she would ask what he had done while there. "I did not go for the sake of accomplishment," he would say. "Only for the pleasure to be where it is so beautiful."

Señor Ramos did not live long enough to know that his land lay on the southern edge of what they call the mother lode, which is where the most gold is! But later, when mines were established there, they made my mother wealthy. It continues to be mined, this land that belonged to Señor Ramos, and it continues to reward those whose mines are located there.

"But," my mother said, "owning a mine is not

as simple as it may appear. If it is at all profitable, claims will be staked and there will be no end of trouble between those who came there first and claim jumpers. It would have made my husband sad," my mother continued, "but it belongs to me now and, as I must do what I can to protect it, I have no time to be sad."

She was silent for some minutes and then, in a softer voice, she said, "One day I shall take you to see the land that was his. It is my hope, Eldora, that you will come to love it. As he did, and I do."

I think I would have liked Señor Ramos.

Although we traveled as comfortably as might be, by midafternoon I was bone sore and mind weary. My mother must have realized this, for she leaned toward me and said that in less than one day we would be home.

Home? The word struck painfully on my ears. Home was the pitched-roof house in New Bedford. Home was the corrugated castle. Whatever lay before us was my mother's home, not mine.

I am tired and I miss you,
Eldora

San Pedro, Salinas Valley, California
Saturday, February 1, 1851

Dear Cousin Sallie,

I have had two letters from Luke since arriving in
San Pedro, and one from you. The one from you,
being addressed to San Francisco, was received by
Aunt who then sent it to me. So it was a long time
reaching me. But that is not the reason you have not
gotten a reply, and neither has Luke. Rather, it is
that I am finding it hard to arrange my thoughts for
the writing of them. I have taken up my pen more
than once, set down a few lines, and then put the
page aside. Every thing is as my mother told it, but
I miss Uncle and Aunt and Lucia and Miguel and
even the neighbor who talks too fast and too much.

I think my mother is disappointed in me. I was
shy with the two guests who came to the inn yesterday and I do not know how to behave with the
Mexicanos who work for my mother. They speak

very little English. I think my clothes embarrass my mother. She is planning a fiesta in my honor and, as I will need some thing quite elegant for that occasion, we are to go to Monterey so we can choose fabric for a new dress for me. Monterey is where my mother's dressmaker lives and works, and she will make the dress.

You would think I would be glad about this. Instead it has made me realize that the clothes I brought are poorly suited to my life here.

I think I have not told you about the inn. It was built by Señor Ramos some years ago. Now, like the mines, it belongs to my mother. It is two storeys high and made of wood. On the upper story there is a porch, which is entered by a door from the hallway and runs across the front of the building. It can be quite hot here, especially in the middle of the day, so it is nice that the roof slants down far enough to shade the porch.

The public rooms, my mother's room, and now my room also, are on the lower floor. My room was her sewing room before I came here. An inside staircase leads up to the guest rooms. My mother told me that it is the only inside staircase in the county!

The kitchen is a small, separate building made of adobe bricks as is true of many buildings here. The kitchen garden, which is behind it, is quite large.

The three people who help my mother are Fernanda, Abdulia, and Alberto, the driver of whom I have already told you. I do not know their last names. Fernanda and Abdulia do the cooking and cleaning. They are kind and try to be friendly to me. The same is true for Alberto. In addition to being the driver, he tends the kitchen garden and the orchard. He also cares for our milk cows, goats, chickens, and horses. When visitors need to exchange their tired horses for rested ones, he does that, too. But the mules, which serve many purposes, are his favorites. With his one leg it is all the more surprising how much he is able to do and how willingly he does it.

I am still embroidering the pillow cover that I began with Aunt before we left New Bedford! You might even remember it and that it was supposed to say, "A man's home is his castle." I have not started on that part yet, and I think I will change the saying to "*Mi casa es su casa*," which my mother suggested. I thought it was a good idea. I try to work on it every day and also I do one lesson from a book that Uncle gave me and read three pages of Latin.

I hope I will have a letter from you before long and that it will find me more cheerful when it comes!

Eldora

San Francisco, California
Saturday, February 8, 1851

Dear Eldora,

I hope I am correct in believing that although you have not written to us, you are well and would enjoy to know how we fare, Uncle and I, and also Luke, Miguel, and Lucia.

I am glad to say that Luke has been more kind and thoughtful than, to be truthful, we had anticipated. When I make pies he sets out the table—and he does this without my asking him to do so! Now that Uncle has enrolled some students and found a place to teach them, Luke helps to clear and clean the room and to restore the tables to good order at the end of each day.

Miguel has become a frequent visitor. He has revealed himself to be an uncommonly gifted artist for one who is both young and untutored. Luke continues the instruction in English that you began, and Miguel introduces him to parts of the city unknown to us. When they set out on such excursions I am some times uneasy. Uncle merely jokes that Luke is learning as much about California as is his father—and all without leaving San Francisco! Lucia is shy with Luke but, in her way, quite friendly with me. So, while Luke and Miguel are busy, she often chooses to help me. I think she misses you.

Uncle and I have begun to ask each other how long we shall stay in our "castle" and, should we choose to build a new home, ought it to be of brick or of wood. Both are costly here. One can also have a large, even two storey iron house, but we do not favor it. Uncle wonders if the three little pigs had similar discussions before each went off to build his own house. I remind him that while we have no need to fear a huffing and puffing wolf, brick has the advantage of being resistant to fire. I believe that when the time comes, we shall build our house of brick.

I hope you have not neglected your lessons and that you are obedient to Mrs. Ramos in all she asks. If you are able to write to us, it would bring great pleasure to Uncle and to myself.

I am, as ever,
Your loving Aunt

San Pedro, Salinas Valley, California
Thursday, February 20, 1851

Dear Cousin Sallie,

The fiesta for me was held this past Saturday. It was a large affair and quite elegant. Fernanda and Abdulia worked for several days to prepare the food. The public rooms, which were specially arranged for the occasion, were decorated with colorful banners that Alberto hung at my mother's exact directions.

In the same clear way in which she instructed Alberto, which I now know to be her way, my mother had given instructions to the dressmaker at our first visit. And so my dress was cut, sewn, and finished by the promised date. It is made of cornflower blue silk. I was complimented many times on how charming, becoming, *et cetera*, it was. My mother's dress was of a similar but darker color.

I knew that my mother had many friends and acquaintances but it surprised me nevertheless to see them all gathered in a single room. Some of the guests traveled a considerable distance to attend the fiesta and many, the governor among them, came from Monterey! Some were accommodated here at the *posada*.

Three musicians, *Mexicanos*, played without stopping. It looked as if they were enjoying themselves. I was happy to see that, because the guests were all talking to one another and I think they scarcely paid attention to the music.

While the fiesta was going on, a courier arrived with several letters for my mother and one letter, from Aunt, for me. I was eager to read it, but when the fiesta ended, I was so tired I saved it until morning.

I think Aunt took care to tell me about Luke and Miguel and Lucia—not just herself and Uncle—and that they are well. She even joked about how it worries her when Luke and Miguel go on "excursions."

Strange to tell, when I read the letter, it made me sad, not happy. I think it reminded me that here in San Pedro every one is new to me. Even my mother is new to me, as I do not remember how it was before I was put to Aunt and Uncle. I would like to ask her about that, but I do not know what my questions might be. It is all very puzzling.

I try to be a deserving daughter—and when I write to Aunt, as I intend to do, I hope I will not write such a muddled letter as this one. I think of you dearly and am ever yours.

Eldora

San Pedro, Salinas Valley, California
Monday, March 3, 1851

Dear Cousin Sallie,

This morning I awoke to the sound of wheels in the roadway. The stage does not come at such an early hour and it was too early for a guest to arrive by his own carriage nor was it the sound of a *carreta*. I got up and looked out the window. To my surprise, I saw Alberto standing beside my mother's carriage, and beside him were her trunk and several hatboxes.

My mother's carriage is distinctive, it having been a surprise gift from Señor Ramos. It was made and shipped by an excellent firm in Massachusetts, she told me with pride.

As my mother had not said we were to go any where today, I rapidly concluded that she intended a journey and that I was not to accompany her. The trunk, hatboxes, and awaiting carriage made it equally clear that she meant to stay a while and that she would need to be properly dressed. If this were not the case, she would choose to ride one of her favorite horses. I was frightened to think that I was to be alone—which is to say without her—in San Pedro and dressed quickly.

I found my mother seated at the dining table. She was perfectly dressed as she always is, and had already eaten most of her meal.

She looked up when I entered. "Oh, Eldora," she said. "I have had a message that some thing quite unfortunate has occurred at one of the mines and I must attend to it. It should take no more than several days, but one can never be certain about these things. Let me say, rather, a week at most!"

Perhaps she observed the dismay I could not hide, for she added, "That is not so very long, Eldora. And you will be well cared for."

A week! She seemed to think it less than a little while. To me it sounded like a very long time.

"Ah, Eldora," my mother said, "I believe you will find, as I have, that unexpected circumstance is the best of teachers. But now I must go. Remember to ask Abdulia for food and Fernanda for all else. I know you will behave yourself until I return."

A few minutes later she was gone.

I was still listening to the sound of the carriage wheels when Fernanda appeared.

"*¡Vamos!*" she said. It was a word that Miguel had said more than once to Lucia, and I remembered her reply.

"*¿Adónde?*" I asked.

Fernanda has a beautiful, wide smile, and she smiled when I said this. I think it was the first time she heard me use Spanish words. Then she held out her hand, meaning that I was to come with her, and led me to the kitchen garden, where two baskets, both of them well used, were waiting at the head of a row. She gave one to me and took the larger one for herself.

Still not saying any thing, she commenced to pick vegetables, and I followed her example. As we passed down the rows, Fernanda named the vegetables that we were picking and it was clear that I was to repeat what she said after her. This occupied us for quite some time and, for what remained of the morning, I busied myself with the Latin and the lesson, and then it was time for dinner. Abdulia had set my place at the table as usual. But Fernanda, guessing that my mother's empty place might be hard to bear, asked if I would like to take my meal with her, Alberto, and Abdulia. I did so gladly.

I commenced this letter immediately afterward. The sun is past its highest, but still it is very warm. I believe I will prepare this letter for the post and then I will try to explain to Fernanda that I wish her to mail it for me and then I will take up my embroidery and after I have worked on it a while, it will be time for our supper and then the first day will be over. I think tomorrow will not be quite so difficult.

Ever yours,
Eldora

San Pedro, Salinas Valley, California
Saturday, March 15, 1851

Dear Cousin Sallie,

It was a full week before my mother returned. As you may imagine, I was glad to see her. She said she had me always in mind, and she brought me three gifts. There was trouble at more than one of the mines and she brought me a gift from each of the places where she had stayed. The first gift was a pair of silk gloves knit in the finest stitches you can imagine. The second was a set of colorful ribbon bows for my hair. The last parcel was the best—a copy of *The Scarlet Letter*. Aunt had liked the book very much, but I was not permitted to read it because, she said, it was not for young eyes. I told my mother what Aunt had said, but she did not seem to have such concerns.

"Well," she said, "those New Englanders are some punkins!" and we both laughed at the expression she chose to use.

Afterward, I was ashamed of myself for laughing at Aunt, even though she is not here and it was my mother who joked about New Englanders, not me. As you know, Aunt's family is like your family in that both families have lived in Massachusetts for more than a hundred years. So if that is how Aunt thinks, it is not surprising, and not funny, either.

The next day

It is nice, having my mother back again, but I cannot tell you what we do or why it is that what I do seems so different when she is here, or why it is that whatever I do does not seem the same.

I have become accustomed to having Abdulia and Fernanda cook, serve our meals, and clean our rooms, as well as those occupied by guests. Fernanda even makes my bed!

Even if my mother is away, travelers to Monterey, or places farther south, may stop here. It is an inn, after all, and "the *posada* of the *señora*" is well known. But if my mother is here, it is very much nicer for the guests, who take their meals with us. Usually the talk is about ranching. Some times they will bring news from San Francisco, which she is always eager to hear.

If I am present, my mother introduces me. "I would like for you to meet my daughter," she says. And then I am to smile, nod, and drop a brief curtsy. But I am not expected to linger.

Once, when a guest exclaimed that he did not know "the *señora*" had a daughter who was so *encantadora* (that means "charming and beautiful"!) my mother smiled and laughed.

"One does not know every thing," she said. And then she changed the subject.

On days when there are no guests, and if my mother does not have to take care of her accounts, she reads, or does needle work. I do my lessons and my embroidery.

Some times my mother's friends call and they sit on the porch and talk and Abdulia might serve them some thing cool to drink. If my mother is to call on others, Alberto will choose a horse for her. But if I am to go too, he will take us in the carriage. This afternoon my mother told me his story.

My mother's husband was in the United States army in the war between Mexico and this country. Alberto, who was on the Mexican side, was injured in a gunfight with Señor Ramos's division. When my mother's husband found him, he saw that this enemy soldier was young, badly injured, and in great pain. Señor Ramos had the thought that it would be easy to kill him and perhaps it would be kind to end his suffering. But he could not find it in his heart to do it. Instead he lifted the man onto his own horse and brought him to the field hospital, where the sorely wounded leg was amputated.

"Señor Ramos did not see him again," my mother said thoughtfully, "and of course he had no way of knowing what had become of the man whose life he had saved. I believe that if my husband gave the matter any further thought, in all likelihood he concluded that if the man had not died in the hospital, he was probably put in prison."

For a while, we continued our walk in silence. Alberto was working in the garden when we passed it. My mother nodded to him but they did not speak, and it would not have been right for me to say something when she did not. But some day I would like to tell him how sorry I am about his being hurt in the war, and that I often think how he still does so much work and is kind to other people.

Presently, my mother told me the rest of Alberto's story. After the war, he made his way to *"el rancho del coronel bueno"*—the ranch of the good colonel. There he found my mother, who then had the sad obligation to tell him of her husband's death. My mother had never asked Alberto how he found the ranch, and there was no need to ask what he meant to do once arrived. He meant to stay and to take care of the land of the *coronel*, and if *la señora* had need of help he would do that too. In the name of her husband she thanked and welcomed Alberto.

I was thinking about this when, quite suddenly and with a bitterness I had not heard before, my mother said, "All of us who live here do not doubt that it was a foolish war, perhaps a wicked war. But death is not concerned with the righteousness of a war. Regardless of their loyalties, soldiers are wounded and die, and others not of the military lose their lives as well."

When my mother fell silent I imagined—correctly as it turned out—that she was choosing what to tell me next. When she spoke again it was to say that with the war over, and her husband no longer among the living, there were many who encouraged her to return to Pennsylvania, where members of her family still lived. "But," she said, "Octavio loved this land and built this inn, and I stayed on. For him."

"It is odd," she added, "how things come about. Had I followed their advice, the gold that was found on Octavio's land would not have been mine and, quite possibly, I should never have found you. So you see, my Eldora of the golden hair, in that regard at least, it was for the best."

Tomorrow we are invited to another fiesta. It is in honor of the commissioner of education for the state of California, and I will again wear my blue silk dress. It seems a pity that I, not Uncle, will meet him. Some times I am brought to wonder why I am here at all.

When I chose to come to San Pedro and the *posada*, I thought my life would be a fairy tale and that I would be a princess with a fairy-tale queen for a mother. Now I am learning that her life has been sad in many ways, and I am beginning to realize just how lonely a princess can be.

Eldora

San Pedro, Salinas Valley, California
Wednesday, April 16, 1851

Dear Cousin Sallie,

This morning my mother surprised me by asking, "Do you know what day it is?"

I was intent on the book I was reading and scarcely looked up as I replied that it was Wednesday.

"Well, yes," she said, "Wednesday. And beyond that?"

"April sixteenth?" I ventured, wondering why she continued to question me in this way and curious enough to set aside my book.

"Quite so," she said, seating herself on the bench beside me. "April sixteenth. It is a very special day, Eldora, though I suppose you could hardly know that it was on this day, exactly fourteen years ago, that you were born."

"It was?" I asked, sounding rather foolish, even to myself.

"It was," she repeated. "And quite possibly the happiest day of my life, and your father's, too."

Aunt had told me often enough how my mother had died, but never any thing about my father, and I had never asked. So when my mother asked if I would like her to tell me about him, of course I nodded.

"To begin with," she said quietly, "he was very tall, strong of jaw, and about the funniest man I ever knew. He could walk into just about any gathering and set the whole room to laughing—not by telling jokes but in the special way he saw things and told about them. He was kind to people, and he loved adventure—"

"Is that why . . . ," I interrupted.

She understood my meaning. "Yes," she said. "That is why he went to California—though not until you had learned to walk and to call him Papa when he rode you on his knee."

I had never thought about the time before my mother sent me away, and I was astonished at this information! "He really did that?" I asked. "And I really called him Papa?"

"You most certainly did," she said, "and when he left us to go to California, you cried and cried and called his picture 'Papa' and some times kissed its face. I would write to him about all the funny things you did and when he wrote to me, he would make funny pictures for me to give to you."

"But if he cared for us so much, why did he go away?"

"It was about trading for hides," she said. "He believed it would make us wealthy. Perhaps that was a bigger reason than the adventure it offered. At that time many factories were starting up in New England, where we lived, and those that made shoes needed leather, and leather is made from hides such as could be had in California. I think," she added, "Mr. Dana's book had some thing to do with your father's decision."

That was one of the books she had encouraged me to read but without giving the least little reason why I should do so. Now I knew.

"One day," she continued, "I received a letter from your father in which he said that California was a beautiful place and that he wished to share it with me, with us. I did not think twice. I loved and trusted him entirely and began my preparations at once. As soon as I could make the necessary arrangements, we left for California, you and I together."

Then, without concluding my birthday story, my mother fell silent. I thought she had lost her way in the telling of it but I believe it was only to set her mind on what she meant to tell next.

"You know," she continued, "every year, every single, single year, I have thought of you on your birthday. And every year I have wished that I had thought to tell Captain Shipman that April 16th, 1837, was your birthday so that it would not go unremarked. And then I would remind myself that I had thought you would be with your father and—"

At this moment Fernanda appeared. "*Señora,*" she said, "*¿Señora?*" She reported that a gentleman of distinction, "*muy distinguido,*" had arrived and that he had come for the exact purpose of seeing my mother. She hesitated only long enough to tell me that we would talk later. Then she went with Fernanda to greet the important guest.

When she returned, the gentleman was with her. They were talking in a very lively fashion, and he had accepted my mother's invitation to take supper with us and stay the night at the inn.

There are times when I wish my mother would not invite every one who comes to the inn to join us at a meal! When I once spoke out about this, she replied that that is how she finds out what is happening in the valley and beyond, and that it is very important for her to do this.

On this occasion I was especially disappointed because she had just told me that it was my birthday, and I would have liked my mother to be with me and not this stranger. Also, I wanted to ask if she still has the picture I used to call "Papa," because I would like to see it. And I wanted her to tell more about me and my father.

But there was no use thinking about such things. A new guest had arrived at the inn and all attention was turned to ensuring that he felt welcomed. I could see Alberto, with his one leg, leading the gentleman's horse to the pasture gate, and Fernanda, standing beside my mother, was ready to lead the guest to his room.

If my mother tells me more about my father, I will tell you.

If I were to tell Aunt that April 16th is my birthday, do you think she would write it on the page in the Bible where other important dates are written, like the day when she and Uncle were married? Or when Henry, their son, was born and when, still an infant, he died? Or when Captain Shipman brought me to stay with them? Now I would like Aunt to write April 16, 1837, on that page. But I will never, ever ask.

Friday

One thing I meant to tell you is that just before Fernanda came to tell about the guest that had arrived, my mother pointed toward the yellow flowers just beyond the edge of the kitchen garden.

"Look," she said, "wild mustard. Can you imagine that there are places to the north where, each spring, it covers entire fields? We do not see that here, I regret to say. But even a few blooms suffice."

Señor Ramos had once taken her to see that springtime display, she said, and now she would like to show it to me. It was not only for the wild mustard and Señor Ramos but because my father had written about it when he had first come to California. It was, he had said, more golden than gold itself, and it reminded him of the color of her hair. If my hair was to become the color of hers, he had added, they had named their child well.

I think I will end this letter here, and I think you will guess the reason.

Eldora

San Francisco, California
1851

Oh my dear Eldora!

Such sad news as was brought to us yesterday in the evening. Miguel has been killed. I would give the world were it not so, but being so, must be told.

A miner, believing Miguel to be an escaping thief, shot him in the back. There were several witnesses to this dreadful act. Indeed the murderer—for he is nothing else—is known by his own account, for he has confessed to the deed. But why should he not? In that lawless region he will never be brought to trial, and some will call him a hero and praise him for killing a Mexican.

Luke's Mr. Higgins walked all the way from Roaring Springs to San Francisco so that he, and not a stranger, might bring the report to Luke. As that is a distance of many miles, the compassion of this ragged, unschooled man moves us nearly to tears.

I believe that Luke has written to you of his friendship with Miguel. Indeed, it appears that Miguel was drawn to mining by Luke's description of his own experience. But where dreams of adventure shaped Luke's determination to attempt mining for gold, Miguel had a different reason. For many years his mother had talked of her longing for a proper house—one with glass windowpanes and a wooden floor. Miguel believed that the possibility of such a house lay in mining and the gold he would find. He was eager to do it for her sake.

When Luke told us of his friend's intentions, our concerns led us to speak with Miguel, and we did every thing we could to dissuade him. Miguel listened politely. But he was young and his mind was made up. Had not his friend Luke told him of men who became wealthy overnight? He believed he might enjoy similar good fortune, and it became clear that nothing we said could change his mind. After all, he said, Luke had stayed in the diggings and returned safely. He felt certain he would do the same.

As a keepsake, Mr. Higgins had given Luke a knife both valuable and distinctive. It was initialed

C.H. and had been his for many years. Before Miguel left San Francisco, Luke gave him Charley Higgins's knife.

I could not match such generosity, but gave Miguel several of my pies. Uncle presented one of his own shirts, joking that now Miguel would have one to wear and one to wash. Miguel was wearing that shirt when he died.

Uncle and I have called on Miguel's family. They live poorly, as might be expected, with many persons—most of them relatives—crowding a small adobe. Miguel was the oldest son and they grieve deeply.

Before going to the diggings, Miguel told his mother that he would be rich when he returned and then she could have the house of which she had oftentimes spoken. Remembering this deepens her sorrow and I must tell you that I wept with her.

The sadness and poverty in that house is painful. You will want to know that I returned the following day with some items from our larder—potatoes, eggs, sugar, rice, salt—as I perceived that their food supply was small. I fear there is little else we can do and I fear we shall not see Lucia again. She hardly dared to look at us the whole time of our visit and her mother has warned her that Americans do not like Mexicans and do bad things to them.

Luke is broken hearted. He seems to believe that if he had not given Miguel the knife, if Miguel had not been known to be in possession of a knife of such value, then Miguel would not have been branded a thief—and *then*, Luke says, his friend would still be alive and it is all his fault.

We have found no way to comfort him, and I suppose there is none. It is a terrible thing that has happened and it weighs on us all.

I encourage you to reveal all I have written to Mrs. Ramos. She herself has known great loss. She will, I am certain, offer such counsel and consolation as can be extended.

Enclosed you will find a brief letter from Uncle. I wish we might be with you at this time and am, as ever,

Your most loving Aunt

Friday evening

Dear Eldora,

Aunt has bravely told you of Miguel's murder and our visit to his family. I will not burden you with repetition, but I do have a request.

One day, during the time that Miguel was in the diggings, which was after we had observed his wonderful talent, I chanced to visit a shop wherein I came upon a packet of fine paper imported from the Orient. Remembering that Miguel had done his drawing on nothing but cheap foolscap, I purchased the paper and also some artists' pencils. I intended to give them to Miguel upon his return.

I find myself unable to use or dispose of these supplies, and it is heartbreaking to come upon them still wrapped as the shopkeeper gave them to me. I have had the thought that you or, more likely your mother, may know an individual who would make good use of my purchases but who would not, himself, be able to afford such luxury. There is no replacing Miguel. But if I were able to help another young and gifted *Mexicano* there would be some comfort in it, and some value.

It is my impression that—living in the Salinas Valley as you do—you may now, or in the future, be acquainted with such an individual.

Please know that Aunt and I think of you more than often.

E. H.

THE SIXTEENTH LETTER

San Pedro, Salinas Valley, California
Wednesday, May 7, 1851

Dear Cousin Sallie,

It is some time since I have written to you and even now I can hardly bear to take up my pen.

Miguel, who called me Eldora-Eldorado, is dead. He was at Roaring Springs, the mining camp where Luke stayed with his Mr. Higgins. Miguel was shot in the back. A miner who believed him to be an escaping thief killed him but any one who knew Miguel would know this could not be true.

Aunt is the one who wrote to tell me about Miguel, and Uncle also wrote, but I have had no word from Luke. When I received the letters from Aunt and Uncle, I wondered why I had not heard from him. I think it is still too new for Luke, and hard.

As you see, I am only now writing to you.

Aunt's letter and Uncle's were in the same envelope. Although intending to do so, I have not written to them since coming here and was filled with remorse and regret when I saw their dear and familiar handwriting. Imagine, then, how I wept when I read their letters. I read them one after the other and since then have read them so many times I know the words by heart. But I still do not believe what has happened, not all the way.

When I told my mother that my friend Miguel had been killed, she got up from her desk and, without saying any thing, led me into the garden.

That morning it was very beautiful there and nobody was about, not even Alberto, who was working elsewhere. My mother said she had hoped that I would not have to know about such terrible happenings—that people can kill one another for poor or foolish reasons or for no reason at all or because they think justice is being done—and that bad things happen here as elsewhere.

I remembered that if my mother heard others start to tell me about such bad things she would say, in Spanish, "Do not frighten the child." But I could understand anyway.

Now I know the worst thing that can happen and every one is being kind to me, but it does not help because they did not know Miguel and they cannot be sad with me.

Some times, when I think about Miguel being killed, I hate California and the mines and the miners (except for Luke's Mr. Higgins) and the gold that can make people do such things to one another.

In her letter Aunt said that she and Uncle have visited Miguel's family. I would like to be able to see them too, especially Lucia. I do not know if Miguel's family can read very much but maybe I will ask my mother to help me write to them in Spanish. My mother has been gone most of this week but maybe, when she comes back, I will ask her.

Since Miguel was killed, I am scared to be here and I am scared for my mother to be away. When I told her that I was scared, she said I should not worry. Then she smiled and said she is much more likely to be robbed than killed. She has been robbed twice, she told me, so she can say from experience that it is a great deal better than being killed. It is also better, she said, for the thieves. When I asked why this was so she said, "Well, if they rob me they can do it again. But not if I am dead."

I wonder if my father was killed or just died from

sickness. I wonder if my mother even knows, and if she will tell me. Maybe, some day, I will ask.

I hope I have not made you sad by telling you about Miguel and all the rest of these things. But now you know that I am all right, just very sad, and that is why I have not written in such a long time, and am

Ever yours,
Eldora

CHAPTER IV

Luke

APRIL 19, 1851 – AUGUST 28, 1851

As no one blames me but myself,
no one else can forgive me.

LUKE TO ELDORA,
LETTER OF MAY 27, 1851

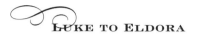

San Francisco, California
April 19, 1851

Dear Eldora,

Mrs. Holt told me she wrote to you about Miguel
being killed. But there are things Mr. and Mrs. Holt
do not know because Charley told me and not them.
One thing is that no sooner had Miguel reached
Roaring Springs than some of the men started in
about the knife he wore on his belt. As you know, it
was not a common knife, and they got to studying
how it came to be the knife of a *Mexicano*, a young
and poor *Mexicano* at that. No one came up with the
idea that it might have been a gift. Then someone,
not meaning any harm or guessing what was to come,
said, "Like as not, he stole it." That settled it for a
good number of the boys, including the miner who
killed Miguel. "Once a thief, always a thief," he said.

So when this miner woke up one morning, and
discovered he had some gold missing from his tent

and then saw Miguel leaving the camp a bit earlier than other days, he just grabbed up his gun and started a chase.

Every one agrees that Miguel must have heard him coming and seen the gun, because he started running—fast—and headed for the river. He was a strong swimmer and when he reached the river, he just dived in.

That is when the man shot him. By then others were with him, chasing and hollering, and by the time they got to the river, Miguel was dead. So they got together and pulled him dead and bleeding out of the water. It was only then that someone thought to ask where was the gold he was supposed to have. The man who'd killed Miguel shook his head. "He must have hid it some where," was the best answer he could come up with. But when he found the knife—Charley's knife, my knife, Miguel's—he just took it. Then they all went back to their tents and made flapjacks.

In the afternoon, Charley told me, he and a couple of miners who had not been part of the chase buried Miguel as best they could and said a couple of prayers.

Two days later, the sack of dust was found. The boys, as Charley calls them, scratched their heads and said it was a shame and went on with their mining. But Charley asked for a look at the knife.

"Well, what do you know," he said, showing them the initials on the side. "Looks to be my knife, and I'll thank you to give it back to me."

Directly he and a couple of others dug up the grave where they'd buried Miguel, and buried the knife alongside, and Charley thought that was some thing I ought to know.

You were Miguel's friend too, in fact you knew him before I did. What I cannot put out of my mind is that *I gave him the knife*. Can you ever forgive me for doing that? Right now I cannot forgive myself.

If you were to write me a line or two I would take it most kindly.

Your friend, most truly,
Luke

San Francisco, California
May 27, 1851

Dear Eldora,

I did not open your last letter right away, being greatly afraid that you would fault me for giving Miguel my knife. Today I read your letter. But I had to read it more than once before my mind believed my eyes and that you do not think it was wrong that I gave Miguel my knife, or that it was my knife that got him killed.

Mr. Holt says that as no one blames me but myself, no one else can forgive me. So, he says, I must find a way to do that. He thinks I will, but it will take time and I must not be impatient with myself. Today, because of what you have written, I do not blame myself quite so much. This is not very well said, but I hope you will understand.

In your letter you said that news of the fire on May 5th reached you and that you feared for Mr. and Mrs. Holt and me, being here with them, and also Pa in his hotel. Although the fire was larger than you could imagine, with flames leaping from building to building, our "castle" was at a safe distance. We did worry some about Pa, as we could see that the fire was approaching his hotel. However, we soon learned that he was not in residence when the fire struck and in fact, it was not long before he appeared at our door.

Because of where the Imperial Hotel is located, Pa could not return until the day after the fire, all the while fearing that his clothes, books, and maps might have been destroyed. Fortunately, this was not the case.

There have been many fires since I have been here, but none like that one. We have learned that as many as eighteen entire blocks, and parts of others, burned. Although the ruins smoldered for days, many stores reopened the day after the fire. Mr. Holt says this city is irrepressible if not unstoppable!

Mr. Holt is still doing some lawyering, which he had taken up when his hopes for a school of his own faded. But now he has found a way to begin his school without having a building! A large room at the back of a store that sells dry goods is his classroom, and eleven scholars are now enrolled. In what

Mr. Holt calls a fair exchange, the father of one of them, who owns the store, does not pay tuition and Mr. Holt does not pay for the use of the room.

On days when Mr. Lewisohn does not need me at the store I stand at the back of Mr. Holt's classroom and make sure that the students pay attention. I am older than even the oldest of them, but I learn some thing new nearly every time, and I am almost sorry when the lessons are finished. Mr. Holt makes things a lot more interesting than the teacher I had in Millfield. I did not think a teacher could make such a difference.

I am getting used to being here.

I hope that you will write to me again and I will do the same.

Your friend,
Luke

Now that you have told me about your birthday, I will try to remember it next year. But I will not say any thing to Mr. or Mrs. Holt because it sounds as if you do not mean to tell them, at least not yet. I think Mrs. Holt would be pleased to put your name in the Bible. But you know her better than I do.

San Francisco, California
June 12, 1851

Dear Eldora,

I was very pleased to receive your letter. The same thing you say about remembering Miguel and how he was killed, and then not remembering, is true for me, too. The worst is before I fall asleep and I keep thinking about him not coming back—ever. Or maybe the worst is when I wake up in the morning and think of some thing I should tell him—and then I have to start remembering, all over again, that he was killed.

We have not seen Lucia.

I am sorry to say that Mr. Lewisohn's store was quite badly damaged in the last fire and was not among the stores and other places of business that were able to reopen the following day. In fact, I worked alongside Mr. Lewisohn and his sons for three days and part of the next one, and I can tell you that it was hard, slow work. Before we could even begin the repairs, we had to clear away merchandise that was no longer salable, set aside other items and mark them FOR SALE CHEAP, and remove and then replace a number of broken windows, burned doors, etc. I am hard put to say which was more difficult—the cleaning up or the rebuilding.

Mr. Lewisohn says he was glad to have my help, and for those days he paid me more than when I work in the store. Since I am supposed to pay Mr. and Mrs. Holt for my share of the food, I am glad of the extra money. Mr. Lewisohn says I am a good worker and deserve to be well paid.

When I was working for Mr. Lewisohn before, I was always noticing things about the sons, such as the way they dress, which is that they wear black pants and white shirts cut like their father's. Also like their father is the way they comb their hair, which is that it makes two long curls that hang in front of their ears, and they always wear small, round caps that fit very close to their heads. Now I am so used to these things I hardly notice the ways we are different. I think they feel the same about me. If we notice any thing, it is that we laugh at the same jokes and enjoy playing tricks on one another.

If you were here, I think you would like the mother. She is quite jolly and laughs a lot. (Mr. L. does not. In fact, he is very serious in his manner.) The small, bonnet-shaped cap that Mrs. Lewisohn wears all the time is part of their religion, same as the caps for the men and the older boys (like Mr. Lewisohn's sons) and Saturday being their Sabbath and that it starts on Friday at sundown. To show that it is the beginning of the Sabbath, Mrs. L. lights two candles and there is a small song that she sings (I think it is a prayer). We watch her carefully and are quiet until she is finished. Then they begin their meal, and I say good-bye and go home to be with Mr. and Mrs. Holt.

Once I brought some sausages that Mrs. Holt made. Mrs. Lewisohn smiled and thanked me, and said I must be sure to thank Mrs. Holt for her. But, she said, she would give the sausages to another family, as they, the Lewisohns, are not permitted by their religion to eat pork and their meat has to come from cattle killed in a special way. There are several slaughterers who do that here in San Francisco, so

I guess quite a few Jewish people live here. I had not known about their religion before, never having known Jewish persons in Millfield. Mr. and Mrs. Holt said they had not known any Jewish persons in New Bedford, but they believed some lived there.

From talking to people here, Pa has become quite interested in the government of California now that it is a state. If he is able to do so, he hopes to travel as far south as the capital. It (Monterey) is quite close to San Pedro. So maybe, if he *does* go, he will see you! Mr. Holt said it would be good to stop in San Pedro, as he believes that your mother, through her late husband, knows many of the people who wrote the state constitution.

Well, I think I have gone on long enough, and I hope I have answered your questions. But if I have not done so, please tell me the next time you write.

Your friend,
Luke

San Francisco, California
June 30, 1851

Dear Eldora,

The other day I was looking at one of Mr. Holt's
books—it was an atlas—and he came in and saw
me before I had a chance to put it away. All he said
was that he was glad to see I had an interest in
books—but that next time it would be better if I
asked his permission before removing a book from
the shelf. That was all. No scolding, which I surely
deserved.

A few days later he said he had gotten the idea
that maybe books were interesting me more than
they used to. Then he led me over to his bookshelf
and showed me several books, and we talked some
about them. *Eldorado* is my favorite so far. The
author is Bayard Taylor, and it is about traveling
in California when he was here three years ago.
The book has quite a few pictures, which he also

made, and you can see plainly that San Francisco has grown a lot since he was here! Another book we looked at was *Two Years Before the Mast*. It was written almost twenty years ago. Mr. Holt said that the person who wrote it was not much older than me when he had trouble with his eyes and, for that reason, left college and became a common sailor, which he was for two years. The book he wrote is about the life and hard lot of sailors. Gold had not been discovered yet, and his ship, *Pilgrim*, was going to California to trade for buffalo hides. The third book Mr. Holt took down from his shelf to show me is called *American Slavery as It Is*. Mr. Holt thought my pa probably had the same book, so maybe I had seen it. I was not sure. Well, he wondered, did I know that although his name is not on the cover, or inside the book either, it is not a secret that it was written by Mr. Theodore Weld. I thought about that but could not guess his reasons. When I asked Mr. Holt about it, he said, as if it explained every thing, that the author was a famous abolitionist. If I wrote a book, I would want people to know I was the writer!

I believe my last letter told about the fire and

Mr. Lewisohn's store. So I think that you will be interested to know that when we repaired the store, we also made more selling space. So Mr. Lewisohn is now offering kettles, pots, tableware (including dishes made in China), and other things for people intending to remain in California. The store used to sell only what miners on the way to the mines might need. You can tell from the things in the store that there are more lady customers these days.

Well, I guess that is all for now. I hope you will write to me.

Your friend,
Luke

San Francisco, California
July 18, 1851

Dear Eldora,

When Pa returned to San Francisco on account of his ankle, he told every one that he still meant to complete his journey. It was to take him through the northern part of the state, through the redwood forests, and perhaps as far north as Fort Ross, which is on the coast. Now, with many regrets and some advice from his doctor, Pa has decided that it would be "unwise" to undertake such a long and arduous trip. Mr. and Mrs. Holt (and others as well) were glad to hear this.

After studying many maps and making a great number of inquiries, Pa has come to the conclusion that Monterey—which he has mentioned before— would be a suitable destination. Pa believes he will be able to travel the distance on foot. But he has been told that it will be possible to procure horses along the way, should this be necessary.

One evening, as Pa and I and Mr. and Mrs. Holt sat outside of the castle, Pa took the opportunity to tell us about his plans. At the very end he added that he hoped I might travel with him! Here he made a point of saying that we would probably pass through San Pedro on the way to Monterey. He therefore intends to write to your mother to ask if we might stay one night, or perhaps two, at the *posada*!

On hearing this, Mr. Holt sent a wink in my direction. "I think," he said, "your pa is meaning to persuade you to accompany him."

If that is so, he has found the right argument, for I would like to see the inn and I would like to see you. Maybe traveling together would go better than when we went to Stockton and I got tired of seeing only what *he* wanted to and also I was impatient to begin mining.

If Pa truly means to travel to San Pedro, and if he does not change his mind about me going with him, I would like that. But first I would have to ask Mr. Lewisohn if it would be all right for me to be gone for several weeks, maybe longer.

Did they celebrate the Fourth of July in San Pedro, or maybe you went to Monterey. Here in San

Francisco it was just the same as in Michigan (and probably where you come from) only bigger! Cannons and rifles were fired from early morning on, flags were waved, and patriotic speeches could be heard from every street and corner. But a big difference between here and Michigan is that it was the first time California got to celebrate the Fourth of July as a *state*. (Michigan got to be a state in 1837, as our teachers were always telling us.)

I had hoped to have a letter from you by now, but none has come. Are you all right? Did I write some thing I ought not to have written in my last letter? If that is the case, please write and tell me so I can explain or apologize, whichever would set things right.

Your friend,
Luke

San Francisco, California
July 31, 1851

Dear Eldora,

When I told Mr. Lewisohn about wishing to travel to San Pedro with Pa, he told me that he has been thinking how to tell me that probably he and his family will not remain in California much longer! This surprised me, as he has added so much merchandise to his offerings, but then he explained that he has had an opportunity to sell his store to another merchant at a goodly profit.

Mr. Lewisohn says he will be sorry to leave San Francisco, but Mrs. L., who has never stopped missing her family, is happy about the new plan. If the sons have their own, or different, opinions in the matter, they were not told to me.

I think the fires have a lot to do with it too, and the looting that follows. It is rumored that many fires are set by vandals. Mr. Lewisohn says, it is his impression that Jewish merchants are more often the victims than others. Because of the fires, several of their friends have lost their homes, or places of business, or both.

Whatever the reasons, I will be sorry when Mr. Lewisohn and his family leave. Moses, the oldest son, and I have become quite good friends. Not as good as with Miguel, but we have explored parts of the city together. He says he feels safe to be with me because I do not in any way look like the son of a Jewish shopkeeper, and I am glad because he speaks Spanish well.

When Moses said we must be sure to write to one another, I reminded him of all the miners' letters I had written when I was at Roaring Springs. It was good practice, I said.

Mrs. Holt has come to ask if I will help her to put away the pie table, as we have come to call it. The sign you made when she started to sell her pies is the one she still uses. It makes me think of you, and I think it reminds her of you too. I thought you would like to know that.

Your friend,
Luke

The next day

As I have not sealed or posted my letter, I will add some good news. Yesterday evening Pa came by to tell us that he has had a letter from your mother. "As they say here," she wrote, "*mi casa es su casa.*" And she will gladly welcome us.

Pa is very much pleased that we will be able to stop in San Pedro and that we will stay at the inn. So am I.

Pa still has some business to attend to here in San Francisco, but we expect to be able to leave on Tuesday or Wednesday. Pa means to make the trip on foot, at least as much of it as possible. I would prefer that to riding as I do not like horses especially.

I will be glad to see you and have begun to look forward to our travels.

Your friend,
Luke

FROM SAN FRANCISCO TO THE SALINAS VALLEY: EIGHTY MILES ON FOOT

BY JOHN HALL

Although my travels to the north had been cut short by my injury, I remained convinced that there was no better way to acquaint oneself with a region than to traverse it on foot. My son, who had agreed to accompany me, approved my decision to walk as much of the distance as we were able. Others assured me that it would be a simple matter to locate horses, should riding become necessary.

Warned that a daytime temperature of 98 degrees Fahrenheit was typical and 110 degrees not unusual, we kept the weight of our packs as light as possible while yet allowing ourselves some few choice items.

Into my son's pack went a change of clothes, including a purple shirt of which he is fond; into mine went a corduroy suit and a linen shirt. Into his went a map and a compass; into mine went a notebook, two pencils, a supply of quills, a penknife, and a bottle of ink. Into his pack went several pies contributed by a friend; into mine went a loaf of bread and a flask of water. At the last minute each of us added a new tin cup. The style of this particular cup is very popular with miners, as its rounded rim and well-shaped handle assure comfort when drinking hot liquids. Convinced that the cups lent a jaunty appearance to our possessions, we fastened ours securely to the outside of our packs.

To a large degree we followed the route taken by Mr. Bayard Taylor several years since and described by him in *Eldorado*, his new and excellent book. Thus in his footsteps, we toiled up mountainsides and were rewarded by views of the spacious valleys below. The heat of the season was exactly as he described, and we made good use of our cups in drinking plenteously from the streams along our path.

There were few settlements but rather many ranches. These are owned, or occupied, by former soldiers, early settlers, and Mexican *rancheros*. Without exception the *rancheros* were kind and generous. Such food as they had—melons, beef freshly slaughtered and skillfully roasted, tortillas, and the like—was freely shared. Our sole hardship was the presence of stubborn and carnivorous fleas in every bed offered. The difficulty, nay the futility, of obtaining a good night's sleep need not be described.

From the *rancheros* we gained the distinct impression that as California's population increases, its requirements change. For example, newer Californians prefer beef from cattle raised from stock brought from the eastern states to the free-ranging, and thus less tender, beef raised here. On the other hand, fresh produce is much in demand. Our informants believe that before long agricultural use of the land will dominate the pastoral use that presently prevails.

Our journey occupied the better part of five days, and most of the way we walked. On the final day we accepted to travel with a *ranchero* in his *carreta*. This is a two-wheeled wooden cart much in use here. It is of heavy construction and drawn by oxen. We might have traveled faster on foot, but in truth we were grateful to cover the remaining distance in relative comfort.

San Pedro, Salinas Valley, California
August 28, 1851

Dear Mother,

Pa and I have been here two weeks! San Pedro is very different from San Francisco, and that is not only because San Francisco is a city and this is a small village with two inns, a few houses, and a crossroad—which is why it is a good location for an inn.

Eldora's mother, Mrs. Ramos, owns the inn, which was started by her husband, who died. Our room is on the second floor and very comfortable.

Pa has gone to Monterey, as he had planned, and was grateful that Mrs. Ramos offered him the use of her carriage. Monterey is the state capital, and it is where they had the convention to write a constitution for the state. Pa hopes to talk with people who took part in the effort. Mrs. Ramos (most people here call her Señora Ramos), knows quite a few people in Monterey. That will make it easier for Pa to meet them.

Eldora's mother is also not here. Cattle—some of which are hers—have been getting into fields that are planted. Some of the fields, like some of the cattle, are hers, but others belong to others. Either way, Eldora's mother has to help decide what should be done. They are finding it hard to make fences that will keep the cattle out. Alberto, who works for Eldora's mother, told me that cattle used to have the land pretty much to themselves. But now there is more money to be made from crops than from cattle. So naturally, no one likes to have their earnings eaten by hungry cows!

Eldora says that her mother is away quite often. She is getting used to it, she says, but I think it is hard for her. The three *Mexicanos* who work for her mother attend to whatever Eldora needs. Their names are Fernanda, Abdulia, and Alberto. The first two cook, clean, and do laundry for the people who stay at the inn. Alberto, who has a wooden leg, looks after the orchards, the kitchen garden, the hogs, goats, sheep, cattle, and mules. The mules are his favorites. The horses do not need much looking after, as they are pastured until someone needs a horse. I have noticed that the matched team for the carriage that Eldora's mother travels in, and one horse that lets her ride but no one else, get special attention!

Alberto and Señor Ramos were both in the war with Mexico but on opposite sides. When Alberto, who was on the Mexican side, was wounded, Señor Ramos, who was an officer in the army of the United States, saved him. When the war ended, Alberto came here. Some times he helps Fernanda, but Abdulia chases him out of the kitchen!

As you have probably guessed, I did not sit down to write this letter just to tell you about Alberto and the others or even about Pa being in Monterey. It is about me, and that I would like to stay in California and go to Mr. Holt's school. I have not told Pa about this because I have just made up my mind these last few days and he is not here. When he comes back, I will tell him.

I think you know that when Pa and I first came to California, Mr. Holt suggested that I attend his school. I did not do it because I meant to go to the mines, and that is what I did, and I am not sorry because I learned a lot, and not only from Mr Higgins.

I think you also know that when I came back to San Francisco, and then when Pa was waiting for his ankle to get better, I stayed with Mr. and Mrs. Holt. I got to know Mr. Holt better than when we first came, and one thing I would do was help sweep out the schoolroom after the scholars left. One day, while I was doing that, I told Mr. Holt about how the schoolmaster in Millfield said I was a poor scholar and a bad influence and that I was not welcome in his school. When I was finished telling about this, Mr. Holt looked at me, gave me a quick smile, and said he guessed that had set me back some.

The way Mr. Holt smiled when I told him about that, and the way he talks to me about books and is interested in what I might say about them, have given me the idea that Mr. Holt does not have such a bad opinion of me as the schoolmaster did.

About me attending his school, I know how to help him some, like filling the water buckets and cleaning the blackboard, and I think that if I added on some other chores (and some for Mrs. Holt) I might not have to pay as much as the other scholars. Also, I have my gold dust to help pay for it. Also, when I am back in San Francisco, I can work for

the man who bought Mr. Lewisohn's store. Mr. Lewisohn said that I was one of the best clerks he ever had. Maybe that is not saying very much! But, from having worked there before, I know where the merchandise is kept and how to weigh certain things and measure others and calculate the cost.

I was planning to tell all this to Pa when he came back from Monterey. But now that I have written it all down, I think I will just give him this letter to read. That way I won't get tongue-tied or some thing of the sort, and once he knows what I have in mind, we can talk about it.

Depending on what he says, I will ask him to send this letter to you along with his next letter. I have not told any one about this—not even Eldora. But if Pa says I may stay in California, then I will tell her, and I expect she will tell her mother.

One thing that started me thinking about this is Alberto telling me, and not just one time, that his life would be so different if he could read. There was not a mission school in his village, and *Mexicanos* were not allowed in the other schools. That is still true, and it is why Miguel asked Eldora and then me to teach him. I think about Miguel a lot. If I were to be a

teacher and could teach other *Mexicanos*, I could tell myself that I was doing it for him.

Another thing that has been on my mind is that Miguel got killed because he was Mexican. California has laws and lawyers, but none that kept him safe. If I could get to be a lawyer, maybe I could change those laws.

So those are the things I have been thinking about, and now that I see them all written down, it is a lot. I hope you are not tired of reading it. If Pa agrees that I may stay here, one thing is certain. I will have a lot to tell about when I come back to Millfield!

From your son,
Luke

There is some thing else that I have been thinking about. It is your brother, Luke, who drowned when he was about as old as I am now. Do you know what he meant to do when he grew up? Maybe I could be like him in that way, instead of taking dares like the one that got him killed, and you could be proud of me after all.

CHAPTER V

Luke & Eldora

AUGUST 15, 1851 – OCTOBER 14, 1851

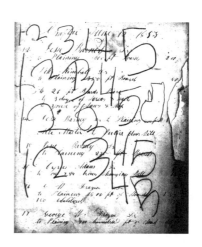

*I think that if you were to meet Luke now,
you would like him!*

ELDORA TO COUSIN SALLIE
LETTER OF SEPTEMBER 12, 1851

San Pedro, Salinas Valley, California
Friday, August 15, 1851

Dear Cousin Sallie,

Luke and his father arrived yesterday, several days sooner than we expected them. *"Mi casa es su casa,"* my mother said with a smile. It is a greeting I have heard often and gotten to know well. But to hear my mother say it, you would think she had just made it up. My mother had said that I must make the introductions. But as it turned out, there *were* no introductions! Before I could give the little speech I had prepared, Luke exclaimed, "Gosh, but you look different, Eldora!" That made every one laugh— including my mother—and it was probably a better introduction than I might have devised.

After the usual greetings were exchanged, my mother summoned Abdulia and instructed her to show Mr. Hall and Luke to the room that would be theirs. Mr. Hall complimented my mother on how well she speaks Spanish, and Abdulia said, "*Sí, señora*," and picked up the packs Luke and Mr. Hall had been carrying. Noting that he seemed discomforted by this, my mother said quietly, "It is a matter of pride and must be respected."

"I can see I have much to learn," Mr. Hall replied.

The next day Mr. Hall expressed an interest in seeing the orchards and vegetable gardens. Fernanda was sent to fetch Alberto, and as soon as he appeared, my mother told him what was wanted and explained to Mr. Hall that Alberto spoke some English, though not a great deal.

Alberto smiled and said, "Good morning, *buenos días*," and Mr. Hall said, "*Buenos días*, good morning," and my mother excused herself. That left Luke and me.

I was glad to see him. But after he told me that he had seen Lucia but only on one occasion, and I asked after Aunt and Uncle, neither of us knew what to say next.

I was the one to break the silence. "It's true, isn't it," I said. "I am not ever going to see Miguel again. Maybe," I went on, "what makes it so hard—us being together—is that it is the first time we have seen each other since . . ."

But then my voice broke, and it remained for Luke to finish my sentence. "Since Miguel was killed," he said quietly. "And it's true."

After that we fell silent again. But now the silence was companionable, not awkward. So when he said, "It's pretty here," I asked if he would like to see San Pedro, and he said that would be nice.

"San Pedro is a very small village," I apologized, "so there is not very much to see."

"But it is where you live," he said.

So we set off.

I led the way until the street turned into the road, the *camino real*, which the Spanish made to connect the missions they established. Along the way we walked past several small houses—all of them adobes—where the *Mexicanos* live, and I pointed out the large house of our nearest neighbor, an elderly and rather cross individual. He is a proud Californian and keeps to himself. Fernanda told me that two of his sons were killed in the war, and it does not make him happy that California now belongs to the United States.

The sun was high by the time Luke and I returned to the inn. The table was set for dinner with my mother's best china—Abdulia's idea of what was proper as we were entertaining guests—and we ate and talked in a rather formal manner.

Monday, August 18

Preparations began this morning for the fiesta in honor of Mr. Hall that my mother proposed. It is to be held on Saturday. When Mr. Hall asked if a fiesta was the same as a fandango, my mother said, "No, not quite. A fandango is for dancing, a fiesta is a large party with music and decorations and food! It is a very cheerful event and very much the custom here." Then she added that it would provide Mr. Hall with an opportunity to meet several of her husband's friends. Among them are some who helped to draft the state constitution. Mr. Hall is most appreciative.

It is good that Luke brought his purple shirt, as we are expected to be present.

As you can imagine, it is very different now that Luke and his father are here and a lot more interesting. Mr. Hall asks many questions, and my mother enjoys talking with him. In this short time he has learned more about this place than I have learned in all the time I have been here!

It is not Luke's way to ask questions, but from time to time I find myself explaining things I had not really thought about knowing about San Pedro! It is better than being by myself, but as you may imagine, I am hard put to keep up with my lessons and have less time for writing letters. Please be patient!

It has been arranged that when Mr. Hall goes to Monterey, Luke will stay here. My mother laughed when she told us that Fernanda and Abdulia do not think it is right for Luke to be here without his father, given my presence in the house, and they have told her so. My mother said she assured them that she will take full responsibility for Luke and, she added with a smile, she has every confidence that he will be an admirable guest. I hope she is right.

Eldora

San Pedro, Salinas Valley, California
Wednesday, August 27, 1851

Dear Cousin Sallie,

Will you be as surprised as I was to learn that Luke wishes to remain in California when his father returns to Millfield? Luke will probably have to live in San Francisco (which he does not like as much as here), as there is no school for him here, and he means to continue his schooling. Alberto, who was the first person to whom Luke told his plan, said it is *"más importante"* for him to return to school. Luke told me next.

I no longer remember how it was that Luke came to tell me that he is named after his mother's brother. The first Luke died when his mother and her family still lived in New Hampshire. Friends dared him to cross a flooding river, and he accepted the dare, and drowned.

I said I could guess how sad that was because

of the sad things that had happened in my family, like my father being dead and the sea captain, Aunt's nephew, bringing me to live with her and Uncle after their infant son died. Yes, Luke said, he already knew about that, and yes, it was sad too.

Mr. Hall came back from Monterey this afternoon. He brought many messages for my mother from people in Monterey. Naturally enough, there were no messages for Luke, but Mr. Hall wanted to know if he had been well behaved and not gotten into trouble. Luke said "Yes, sir" and "No, sir" to his father's questions, and then he said there was some thing he wanted to talk about with his father.

Mr. Hall said that in that case he supposed he had better listen. Well, yes, Luke said. But he had written it in a letter to his mother. But it was really for both of them. So perhaps his father should read the letter and then they could talk. That is what they are doing now—reading the letter and talking about it. I am glad Luke told me beforehand, and I hope Luke's father says he may stay. I wish it could be here, in San Pedro, not San Francisco.

When Luke told me about writing a letter to his

mother but not sending it, I could not help but ask, "Why not?"

"Well," he said, "there's no use scaring her half to death with worrying about some thing that might not even happen." I could not help but think that the way he said it, he was sounding just like Aunt. After all, I told myself, it is his family and I suppose he knows not to tell them things they might not like to hear.

Abdulia is calling me to help her in the kitchen. She had not expected Mr. Hall's return today, so now she must prepare a larger and fancier meal. It is too bad he arrived too late to partake in the one we enjoyed earlier—it was delicious! I will continue this letter tomorrow.

This morning, after we had breakfasted, Mr. Hall went to his room to do some writing. He said it was important that he prepare a dispatch. "After all," he said, "Monterey is the state's capital and deserves a wide-awake report!"

I think that is true. But Mr. Hall did not come downstairs for many hours, not until we called him to dinner. So I think he was also writing to his wife about Luke's letter.

Mr. Hall did not tell Luke his answer right away. But after we had had dinner and talked about the usual things, he told Luke that he had read the letter and in fact had written his own letter to Luke's mother, though of course neither letter would be posted immediately, and now he would like to speak with Luke. He suggested that they take a walk.

Mr. Hall's expression was so serious I thought he was going to tell Luke that he could not agree to have Luke remain in California and that he was disappointed by what Luke had written.

I was glad, for once, to be wrong!

When they returned from their walk, both Luke and his father were smiling, and Mr. Hall seemed to take great pleasure in telling me and my mother what had been decided.

"I am sure there are many persons here who will be glad to hear that," she said. "And I count myself among them."

So do I!

Eldora

MONTEREY:
CALIFORNIA'S CAPITAL
BY JOHN HALL

The city of Monterey offers the visitor a very different impression than does San Francisco, her younger, larger, and more boisterous sister to the north. Representatives of nearly all the nations of the world are to be found on San Francisco's streets, and the babel of the many languages they speak both charms and confuses the ear. In Monterey one hears but two languages: English and Spanish. They are valued with such equality that the constitutional convention, convened here two years since, was conducted and reported in both languages. The same is true of the final document.

In the region surrounding Monterey many families retain ownership of lands first granted by the kings of Spain and represent the highest order of Spanish aristocracy. When Mexico achieved independence some thirty years ago, ownership of these lands was renewed.

But it is not by its history alone or the refinement of its population that Monterey distinguishes itself.

The city is lively, cultured, politically significant, and prosperous. The region's first theater is located here, and the Custom House is a prominent feature of the harbor and of the regional economy. All ships bound for Californian ports must pass inspection here, and it is here that they pay all taxes and duties levied upon their cargoes.

The variety of items received is truly astonishing. Rice, teas, spices, and other foodstuffs are brought from foreign lands; also window glass, ironware, tableware, tinware, ribbons, and cloth; also the kits described in an earlier communication for both iron and wooden houses. Pianos are much in demand, and like other large items destined for the homes of the prominent and wealthy, they are disassembled for shipping and reassembled on arrival. Shelf clocks, mirrors, damask draperies, and other fashionable furnishings are readily available. Outstanding among the objects received here, and still talked about, was the carriage ordered by Colonel Frémont as a surprise for his wife. It had glass windows and was lavishly decorated. Its well-cushioned seats ensured that she might ride in comfort on California's admittedly rough and rutted roads.

I learned, with some amusement, that many of the shoes received here are made from hides originally transported from California to New England's factories!

There is but one respect in which Monterey's prestige is threatened by upstart San Francisco. This is the latter's proximity to the goldfields. Ships may stop at Monterey to pay their respects to the Custom House; but San Francisco is, increasingly, the destination of passengers and goods alike. It should be noted that San Francisco and Monterey are not the only significant cities in the region. Stockton, east of San Francisco and accessible by boat, has a large and vigorous population. Sacramento, to the northeast, is also growing.

San Pedro, Salinas Valley, California
Monday, September 8, 1851

Dear Cousin Sallie,

The other day Luke showed me a small book he found near Roaring Springs. He had brought it with him to San Francisco, where he used it to teach Lucia her letters, and he brought it to San Pedro because he has grown fond of it. Also, it reminds him, in good ways, of Lucia and Miguel.

Now he is using it to teach Alberto to read! The book seems small and childlike to be a grown man's lesson book. But either they do not notice, or they do not mind. I have seen them together, and it is with ample goodwill that they point to the pictures and name the objects shown.

This morning I was present when Luke encouraged Alberto to tell a small story, in English, about each picture they named. I would not have thought to do that, and it surprised me that Alberto, who is very proud, would agree to do it, but he did.

When the lesson ended, Luke went with Alberto to help with his mules and to learn how to handle them. Luke says it is a fair trade—him teaching Alberto to read and Alberto teaching him about mules. It reminds me of the way Uncle talks, and I think Luke learned that idea from him. When I write to Aunt and Uncle, I will tell them about Luke being a teacher. I think they will be glad to hear it, and I think that if you were to meet Luke now, you would like him! He has changed a lot, being here, and maybe I have too.

The last letter I received from you was about how you are better at spelling than the boys in your class, including that show-off Billy Winslow. But how did you ever know how to spell "syzygy"? I told Luke about it, and he said he did not believe there was such a word. So we looked it up in my mother's dictionary and there it was. It has to do with astronomy, but I guess you know that.

What is Baby Emily able to do now? If you have a picture of me, I hope you will show it to her and teach her my name.

I intend to write again soon.

Eldora

San Pedro, Salinas Valley, California
Thursday, September 18, 1851

Dear Cousin Sallie,

I think that talking about Miguel—which, after that first time, we have done a lot—has helped me and Luke to be friends. Yesterday I was telling him about the sea voyage with Aunt and Uncle and how, when we were becalmed, a sailor passed the time teaching me to tie knots. Luke said that he also had learned knots from a sailor. But which ones? To answer the question, we begged a length of cord from Abdulia and took turns tying knots—half hitch, figure-of-eight, running bowline! He was surprised that I could do them, and I am finding out that he is interested in more things than you would guess from first knowing him.

I am not the only one here who likes Luke. I am beginning to think that every one else does too! He talks about mules, cattle, horses, and sheep with Alberto, and about books with my mother when she is here. When Abdulia serves our meals, she puts the largest portions on his plate, and we all pretend not to notice. As for Fernanda, she is making a shirt for him. Luke brought two shirts with him, but one of them, the purple corduroy shirt he wore at the fiesta, is of little use here, as the cloth is much too heavy for midsummer in San Pedro. Fernanda admires its purple color but says Michigan must be a very cold place for him to have such a shirt!

I must remember to tell Aunt and Uncle about Fernanda and the shirt the next time I write to them. I think they will like to know about it—especially Aunt—and I seem to be having quite a few things to tell about!

Today Alberto said one of his ewes was about to give birth and Luke and I might come to watch or maybe assist. I probably would not have gone by myself—and probably Alberto would not have asked me. But Luke was curious, and so both of us went. It was horribly messy when the baby came out, but I am glad we saw it.

The other day Luke's father was talking with one of the guests. Although I did not mean to listen, I could not help hearing when the guest, who was from Sacramento and obliged to travel a lot, said that my mother was one of California's best innkeepers! Then Mr. Hall said he understood that she was an excellent businesswoman and well respected by the *rancheros*. The guest said he had heard the same, and more than once. I was happy to hear those things, and proud to be her daughter.

Even so, I wish she did not have to be away so much. Some times I wonder if it is a good thing for me to be here. She has so much to do, and she is not used to looking after a daughter. When she has been away an extra-long time, she brings me extravagant gifts and says how dearly she loves me, and I tell her I love her the same, and it is true. But if I need some thing, I will ask Fernanda.

I think my mother misses Señor Ramos a lot. I think she also misses my father, especially now that I am here, but differently. I guess every one misses someone. I miss Aunt and Uncle and you, and Luke has said how he misses his ma.

I am always so happy when I have a letter from you. If there is some thing you would like to know about the inn or San Pedro or the valley, please tell me.

Eldora

San Francisco, California
Tuesday, September 23, 1851

Dear Eldora,

Uncle and I think of you often. I hope this letter, which leaves us in good health, finds you and Mrs. Ramos the same, also Mr. Hall and his son if, indeed, they are still with you in San Pedro. Here in San Francisco there is more sickness than when you were here for the simple reason that there are more people here—more arrivals every day!—and there is a shortage of good living conditions. When I speak to Uncle of my concerns for you, he reminds me that San Pedro's situation is quite different and probably more healthy. Still, I cannot help but worry.

It must be acknowledged that the other side of the coin—and I do mean coin!—is that shops and services of every kind are flourishing. Whether the new arrivals remain for a time or proceed directly to the mines, whether they are sick or well, they all require food and housing and supplies of one kind or another—and San Francisco's merchants, lawyers, doctors, wainwrights, carpenters, and others are eager to meet their needs.

I believe you will be glad to know that Uncle and I have again visited Lucia's family. I had made a dress for her beloved doll some time ago and expected that she would call on us soon and that I would give the dress to her then. But Lucia's visits did not continue after Miguel's death, and at last I concluded that we must seek her out.

Lucia was happy to see us, and her mother was grateful that we came. Uncle has by now learned enough Spanish that he was able to convey our concern for the family and our continued sorrow over the death of her son. He added that you were happy to be living with "*su madre*" in San Pedro.

As we made our way home from our visit, I reminded him that we have not heard from you or your mother in quite some time. So how can we be certain you are happy?

"Never mind that," said he. "If aught were amiss, we surely would know of it. We must trust that she is well. And did you not see how the child brightened when I spoke of Eldora?"

If you were to write to us, and enclose a message or the smallest trinket for Lucia, we will make every effort to see that it reaches her.

Please give my warm regards to Mrs. Ramos and know that I am, as always,

Your most loving Aunt

San Pedro, Salinas Valley, California
Thursday, October 2, 1851

Dear Cousin Sallie,

Since the last time I wrote, I have had a letter from Aunt (I think she worries about me) and my mother has been on another trip about the fences. My mother's trip was shorter than usual and she was cheerful when she returned. She told us that just before it ended, the *rancheros* said that if she had not come, not nearly so much would have been accomplished. She told us that when they first sat down together, she made every one laugh by saying that they would have to talk to one another, as it was of no use to talk to the cows. When she told us about it, *we* laughed! My mother has a way of talking that makes people laugh even if they start out angry. Talking with the *rancheros* was one of the times she did that. I wonder if this is some thing she learned from my father.

Mr. Hall's visit is coming to a close. He has traveled quite widely in the area, usually on foot. On Saturday there is to be a farewell fiesta. The week after that, with Alberto driving my mother's carriage, my mother, Luke, and I will go with Mr. Hall to San Francisco. Aunt and Uncle will join us at the wharf, and we will all say our good-byes to Mr. Hall and watch his ship set sail.

Mr. Hall has met many people, and as he is well liked, a large number of them wish to attend the fiesta. For the past three days my mother has been writing the invitations, Alberto has been going here and there to deliver them, and Abdulia—with several friends assisting her—has been preparing the food. Fernanda has finished the shirt for Luke, and now she helps Abdulia in the kitchen.

My mother's new dressmaker was to make the dress I am to wear for the fiesta. Unfortunately, she did not do the hem in the right way, so Abdulia took out the stitches and pinned it properly. I had secretly hoped that she would sew it for me, but no she said doing the hem of my dress would be good practice for me. I have been hemming ever since as Abdulia insists that my stitches be small and of an exact size.

If they are not, she makes me take them out and do that part again. Otherwise, Abdulia says, I will be sorry every time I wear the dress. Perhaps that is true. But right now I am sorry because, as you know, hemming is the most tedious task you can imagine, and this dress has the biggest and widest skirt!

Luke is helping Alberto to make new fences. They are to replace the old ones, and when Alberto is away delivering invitations, Luke works at it by himself. It is hard work, and hot. Mr. Hall is writing.

When she came back from her last trip, my mother said the inn looked better than ever and that we really do not need her at all. "Oh, no!" we said. "Oh, no, *Señora*! It is all for you, and without you it would be nothing."

October 5th

The fiesta for Mr. Hall was a grand success, even better than the one that welcomed him! Every one said so, and I thought the musicians played more cheerfully than usual, but maybe that was because I was enjoying myself more. Also, Mr. Hall has met, visited, and talked with many of the guests, and they were glad to see him. So there was a lot of laughing and joking and telling him what he ought to put in the articles, which every one knows he is writing. I noticed that Mr. Hall made no promises.

Luke looked, as Fernanda had said he would, *muy elegante* in his new shirt. After a while, with so many people crowded together, it became very warm in the room. Luke and I did not need to be there the whole time, so we stepped outside. It felt good to be away from all those people and the music and candles and people (or did I already say that!) and food. The night air was cool and dark, and when we found ourselves walking in Abdulia's garden, we had to be careful not to trample any thing and make her cross in the morning.

While we were walking, Luke took my hand and held it. I think we were both thinking about kissing, but we did not do it. Afterward I could not fall asleep. I was thinking about Luke, but also about my mother and how every one says she is such a good hostess, and Mr. Hall's saying she is such a good business-woman. She is a good mother, too, but she is away so much and I am always afraid that she might not come back, which is what happened to my father.

214

=

I try to tell myself that she will not need to be gone so much when the new fences are in place. But it is no use. However much I might *wish* it to be so, there will always be claim jumpers and bandits and quarrels with new settlers. They will always need my mother to make jokes about talking to cattle, and she will always want to do what she can to make this place a good place. It is not just for Señor Ramos anymore, but for herself, and how much she loves the land.

I wonder how it will be to see Aunt and Uncle again. It has been many months since I saw them last, and I wear my hair differently now. What will I say to them? What will they say to me? I would like to tell them that often, when I am in San Pedro and I do not know what is the right thing to do, I remind myself of what they would say and how much it helps. I hope I will be able to tell them, but if my mother is nearby and listening, it would hurt her feelings. If Aunt gets one of her cross looks, I probably will not say any thing.

I am glad that Luke will be there, because he can usually find some thing to say no matter who it is. For example, once, when we met the angry man whose two sons were killed in the war, Luke looked right at the man and paid a compliment to his small garden. The next time we met on the road, Luke said, "*Buenos días.*" The man actually smiled at that, and then, because it was already afternoon, he corrected Luke. "*Buenas tardes,*" he said. "*Buenas tardes,*" Luke replied.

Me finding the right thing to say to Aunt and Uncle is not exactly the same as Luke saying "*Buenos días*" and "*Buenas tardes*" to the sad, angry man. But I think you know what I mean.

I am, as always,
Your Eldora.

The Imperial Hotel
San Francisco, California
Tuesday, October 14, 1851

My dear Son,

Day is breaking on this, the day of my departure. In anticipation of the sea voyage ahead of me I have just now written a letter to your mother and firmly, if sorrowfully, labeled it: "To Be Opened Only If I Am Lost at Sea." Yesterday I also wrote a final dispatch for the *Herald.* To ensure that the letter, the dispatch and I, do not sail with the same ship, and thus run the same risks, I shall give both of them to Mr. Holt and ask that he post them separately.

But no such precautions need be taken with this, my letter to you. We will meet in the morning and, with as firm a handshake and as broad a smile as I am able to muster, I will give it to you then.

Now, as we near the brink of separation, I find it even more difficult than I expected to consider that you will soon be some two thousand miles away by land and a six-week voyage by sea. I reassure myself with the knowledge that you will not need my advice concerning your course of study, for Mr. Holt is admirably equipped in that regard.

As for your care and well-being, I have already observed that Mr. Holt's wife is an estimable woman and that she appears to have taken a sincere liking to you. I can only remind you not to take advantage of her affection. I believe it will console your mother, as it reassures me, to bear in mind that Mrs. Holt, the figurative aunt of your friend Eldora, is in fact the aunt of several of your mother's girlhood friends! How large this world! How small!

I wish you always to know that your mother and I have—and always will—love you dearly. Differences and disagreements there surely have been, even harsh words. But I must tell you that I nearly refused to permit you to stay in California for knowing how sadly it will affect your mother and myself. And by what was I persuaded? That there was such honor in your proposal, such seriousness in your purpose, and such clarity in your argument.

I hope that your mother and I may look forward

to faithful accounts of all that befalls—the good, the bad, the satisfactory, and the disappointing. I have come to believe that the person who admits to no error and acknowledges no dismay is either deaf, blind, or a liar.

Well, I believe I have gone on long enough. As I have told you, I intend to disembark at Panama City and to travel by land across the isthmus to Chagres. Once arrived in Chagres, I shall make arrangements for the remainder of my journey.

Wherever I may be, I shall be thinking of you often and fondly. It will please me to believe that, from time to time, you will think not unkindly of your some times obtuse, often wordy, but always devoted father—

J. H.

Halfway to San Pedro
Tuesday, October 14, 1851

Dear Cousin Sallie,

My mother, Luke, Mr. Hall, and I arrived in San Francisco yesterday in the afternoon. We went directly to the hotel where all of us were to stay the night. Quite early in the morning Alberto drove us to the wharf where we would wish Mr. Hall a safe journey and say our good-byes.

Aunt and Uncle joined us there. It gladdened my heart to see them, and their pleasure at catching sight of me relieved any doubts I may have entertained. But then I remembered that when Luke was teaching Miguel, and Miguel wrote the only letter I ever had from him, he said it would be good if I were to visit. It made me sad to think I had not done so.

Aunt had written some time ago that Lucia visited them from time to time, and I wanted to ask if she still did so, and if she brought No-Name when she came, and if the miner who had been our first customer still bought Aunt's pies whenever he came to San Francisco. But my mother's presence lent a certain awkwardness to our reunion, and I did not ask any of my questions. As if by common consent we refrained from saying how happy we were to see each other and spoke rather formally of the weather and the excellent appearance of the ship on which Mr. Hall was to sail. Luke's evident sadness as the moment of parting approached was cause for further restraint.

Did Luke, at this last minute, regret his decision to remain in California? He watched intently as his father stepped into the dory that would take him and several other passengers to the waiting ship. Once they were seated, the sailors positioned their oars and, at a signal from the ship's officer who accompanied them, began to row.

If I found myself wondering about the letter Mr. Hall had given to Luke at the last moment, how much more curious Luke must have been! But neither of us said any thing of the sort. Once the dory reached the ship, and the passengers, his father among them, clambered up the ladder to the deck, Luke presented a more cheerful demeanor. The dory, which was one of several, returned several times, and we laughed and joked until the last of the passengers had been boarded.

Despite the distance, we scanned the bay, hoping—even as Luke—to catch a last glimpse of his father. We were not rewarded in this and had to content ourselves with observing the sailors as they prepared for departure.

Uncle, who does not like good-byes, said we ought to start back up the hill. But Luke wanted to wait until the anchor was weighed, the first sails were set, and *Mary Kate*'s voyage had begun. We all deferred to him, even Uncle, and a good thing it was, too. In those few minutes of delay Lucia appeared in our midst!

Despite its size, San Francisco is little more than an overgrown town. Neighbors talk to neighbors, and as Uncle is fond of saying, talk travels the avenues faster than any conveyance. One way or another, word of my presence in San Francisco had reached Lucia, and she had hurried to find me. Her first thought was that I would be at the corrugated castle. I was not there, of course, and neither were

Aunt and Uncle. But a neighbor, recognizing Lucia's disappointment, told her that we had all gone to the wharf to say good-bye to a friend.

I cannot describe the happiness that shone from Lucia's eyes, or the joy with which I embraced her. She was almost as happy to see Luke, for she had known him as Miguel's friend, and she seemed glad to see the *señor* and the *señora*—meaning Uncle and Aunt. Lucia told Aunt that she was taking good care of No-Name and that the dress was still *muy hermosa*, very beautiful. But she spoke so softly—almost in a whisper—that her words could scarcely be heard, and I wondered if she was remembering her mother's warning about *Americanos*. When I saw that she was curious about the tall woman with golden hair who stood beside me, I told Lucia that it was *mi madre*, which confused her very much. Hoping to clear the matter up, I added that I now lived at the *posada de mi madre* in San Pedro, but that did not help. Lucia understood about a *posada*—in fact, she smiled and said to me, "Hotel?" But it was apparent that she had no idea where San Pedro might be, and I did not know how to tell her. I was grateful to my mother, who offered some helpful words in Spanish.

The others had all been watching me and Lucia, and when we turned back to the harbor, it was to discover that *Mary Kate* was gone from her moorage. We tried to determine which of the several ships now under sail was the one carrying Mr. Hall on his way. But the ships were, to our eyes, indistinguishable, and when we turned back from the waterfront, Lucia was gone.

We did not tarry thereafter. I was sorry that we had not exchanged more than a few words, which were of the most general kind. I believe that Aunt felt the same, and Uncle also.

My mother was gracious, Luke silent. Alberto regarded him with great fondness but said nothing. Luke's belongings being few, he and Uncle agreed that they would be able to carry them to the castle.

All that remained was to say good-bye, which we did with few words, and then my mother and I stepped into the carriage. The horses, being already impatient, needed little encouragement. With a light slap of the reins, they took off briskly.

San Francisco was well behind us when, quite unexpectedly, my mother turned to me and asked that I tell her about Lucia. For the next several miles I described our first meeting, the neighbor's disapproval, and how Miguel would some times come with Lucia.

"And then?" my mother asked. And then, I said, I had gone to live with her in San Pedro, and then Miguel was killed, which she knew, and Aunt had made a dress for No-Name and given it to Lucia.

"No-Name?" my mother asked. So I told how Lucia's doll had gotten its name at our very first meeting.

My mother and I traveled in silence for a time, each of us with our own window to look out of and our own thoughts to occupy us. I was thinking of Luke and how saying good-bye to his father had made him sad. I wondered if he guessed that I was sad to say good-bye to Aunt and Uncle, and that I was not entirely sure *how* I felt about his taking my place in the castle. Every one agreed that it was a good plan. But that did not mean that I must like it, and when he asked if his sleeping corner was still there, and Uncle said it was ready and waiting—in that moment I realized that I did not like his being there at all.

My mother's thoughts led her to a question on quite a different matter.

"Does Lucia not attend school?" she asked.

"No," I said, "it is not possible."

"She seems very clever," my mother remarked, and I nodded.

Just then we came to the place where we are to stay the night. Alberto said it was good to stop—before the horses became overtired and risked injury. It is our hope to reach San Pedro late tomorrow or early the next day.

The *posada* is not nearly so handsome as my mother's inn or even the one where we stayed last night. But the *señor* who owns it is kind and said it was an honor to meet me, and our accommodations are sufficient. My mother is, of course, acquainted with him. I think, as I believe I have said before, that there is no one in this part of the state—perhaps all of California—she does not know!

The innkeeper seemed eager to prolong the conversation, but saying that the events of the morning, and the hours of travel, had wearied us, my mother asked if we might be shown to our room. Now she is resting and I am engaged in writing this letter. Sounds from the kitchen suggest that we will soon be called to the evening meal. Equally certain is that the innkeeper will seat himself near us!

It has been a very long day. If the farewell to Mr. Hall occasioned it, I was unexpectedly affected by seeing Aunt and Uncle again, and the glimpse of Lucia. But what is most clearly in my mind is Luke, with Uncle helping him and Aunt alongside, trudging up the hill toward the corrugated castle. When they were nearly halfway up, Luke halted, turned, appeared to search for a sight of me, and, when he saw me, waved.

I am, as ever,
Your Eldora

CHAPTER VI

Eldora

OCTOBER 24, 1851 – DECEMBER 13, 1851

This is not about cold tortillas!

ELDORA TO COUSIN SALLIE
A RETORT TO HER MOTHER
QUOTED IN LETTER OF NOVEMBER 4, 1851

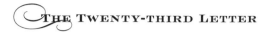

San Pedro, Salinas Valley, California
Friday, October 24, 1851

Dear Cousin Sallie,

Early yesterday morning who should appear at our back door but Lucia and her mother! Abdulia, who saw them first, thought they were beggars and was inclined to send them away. But then Lucia spoke my name and Abdulia relented.

Soon, speaking in Spanish, their story was told and repeated to my mother, who told it, in English, to me. It has been very bad for them since Miguel was killed, and very sad. One by one the other brothers have gone away. Where they have gone, *¿quién sabe?* Who knows? One sister is still in San Francisco, but Lucia's mother would not say where she is or what she is doing. Lucia's father works in the mining camps. He has long been absent. He has sent no messages. If he will return, *¿quién sabe?*

Lucia's mother says that San Francisco is no

longer a good place. Too many *banditos*. Too much fear. Too much remembering what happened to Miguel. She means to go to her village in Mexico. She can do work there, in the fields, and she can eat what they grow. She has friends in her village, and they will make a place for her to sleep. But for Lucia? No. In her village there is *no escuela*, no school, *no esperanza*, no hope. And so, because I have been a good friend to Lucia, and because Lucia told that I am in San Pedro, she has brought Lucia to me.

I think Lucia's mother had not told Lucia why they had come to the inn. Only now, when she looked directly at Lucia and said that the *señora* was good, and the *señorita* also, and that Lucia must do whatever the *señora* asked, did Lucia understand that her mother meant to leave her with us. I saw her eyes widen with fear, and the longing and great love with which her mother regarded her was unmistakable. Then, with a barely whispered "*Adiós, mi hija*," she touched the head of Lucia's beloved doll and began to walk slowly away. And Lucia? She stood without moving, without making a sound. Holding her doll, she watched as her mother reached the street and, still without looking back, turned south toward Mexico.

Fernanda was the first among us to move toward Lucia. Speaking in Spanish, but with words so few and simple I needed no translation, she told Lucia to come with her to the kitchen, *la cocina*.

"I think you are sad and I think you are hungry," she said. "The sadness I cannot take away. But food will help the hunger—"

"No," Lucia said, "no."

"Eldora will come with us," Fernanda coaxed, and I stepped forward to take Lucia's hand.

Once she had been given some thing to eat, Lucia could hardly stay awake. My mother, who had followed us to the kitchen, now told Fernanda to make a bed for Lucia and that it was to be in my room. Fernanda started to object, but my mother shook her head. "Eldora is the only friend that poor child has," she said, "and the only one of us she knows. She will share Eldora's room."

I had not really considered where Lucia would stay or sleep. But I was pleased with my mother's instructions.

This morning Abdulia brought fresh clothes

for Lucia and took away the soiled and dusty ones.
Among those that Abdulia brought I recognized a
skirt that one of her nieces some times wore.

Monday

On Saturday morning several guests arrived,
and my mother seemed pleased to introduce me.
They were interested to learn that I had only
recently come to live with her, but their interest
faded when I was not able to answer their questions about President Taylor's politics and his
death the previous July. That evening there was
a big fiesta that my mother and I were obliged to
attend. Yesterday we met for a Bible reading with
several of her friends. Alberto took us there in the
carreta, and it was a slow ride, about one hour in
each direction. Yesterday, Sunday, I was not able to
be with Lucia very much, but I saw that Fernanda
took time to play a small game with her, and when
Abdulia was making tortillas, she gave Lucia some
of the dough and invited her to make some small
ones for herself.

I think I am learning the most from Abdulia

and Fernanda. Since I have been in California, the greatest kindness has been shown by them and by Luke's Mr. Higgins.

There was one more thing I wanted to tell you about. Last night, on returning to my room and finding Lucia soundly asleep, I lit a candle and took my mother's earrings from their keeping place. I looked at them for a long time, not knowing why I did this. After some minutes a memory came to mind, and I remembered Captain Shipman holding me in his arms, and my mother—my young and beautiful mother—giving one earring to him.

And I remembered that I, like Lucia, did not cry.

Eldora

San Pedro, Salinas Valley, California
Thursday, October 30, 1851

Dear Cousin Sallie,

When I wrote to you this past Friday, I told of Lucia's surprising arrival and that it was my mother who directed that a bed be made for her in my room. I believe that letter is even now on its way.

However, the past week's events give a very different and confusing impression. In the hope that it will help me to untangle my thoughts, and also because I have promised you a true account of all that transpires here, I am writing again.

You must know first that another child has been placed with us—a boy brought here by Alberto. We believe the boy to be a nephew, but it is not at all certain. When pressed for information, Alberto shrugs. *"No sé."*

The boy is named Rafael. He is smaller and younger than Lucia, perhaps four years old. There is

a little chair in the kitchen, and he has made it his own. He neither cries nor talks, neither in English nor Spanish. If we give him a toy, he will just hold it and hold it. He does not play with it, and he does not give it back, which gives an odd feeling. He has been here three days. If Fernanda or Abdulia give him food, he will eat it.

Yesterday I asked my mother why Rafael looks so frightened. She had no idea, she said. "But why," I repeated, "why does he look so frightened? Even if you do not know, what do you *think?*"

My insistence displeased her. "Really, Eldora," she said. "I must ask you to stop asking about Rafael. Life is hard, and for some people it is harder than others. We are among the fortunate ones."

"Even when you were sick?" I asked. "Even when my father died? Even when Señor Ramos—" I was nearly shouting, but I could not help it.

"I must ask you not to continue with these unfortunate questions," my mother said, "and it would be better if you would lower your voice."

Some times I think that all my mother cares about is my being polite, quiet, and obedient.

When Rafael sees my mother, he looks scared.

He knows quite a lot of English, and I try to tell him that no one here will hurt him, but it does not help. He just stares at me with his eyes wide open and not even blinking. If I ask if he would like some thing to eat, he shakes his head. So then I tell him to ask Abdulia when he is hungry. And if he has dropped a toy, I pick it up and give it to him, and then I say, "*Adiós*, Rafael," and go out of the kitchen.

Lucia does not speak to him, nor does he speak to Lucia. They are quiet as shadows.

If Luke were here, he could tell Rafael that he does not have to be frightened, and maybe Rafael would believe him because he, too, is a boy and that strange, sad look would go away.

If I ask Fernanda about Rafael, all she says is that *la señora* knows best. I have not even tried to talk to Alberto about Rafael. I am not sure, because Alberto was speaking in Spanish to Abdulia, but I think he said that it was not "his thought" to bring Rafael to the inn and that another person (His niece?) said he must do so. So now, Rafael spends his days in the kitchen with Abdulia and at night he goes, with her, to her house.

I have had a long letter from Luke, which I will tell you about another time. I seem to have two friends now, you and Luke. But as neither of you is nearby, I can only miss both of you, though differently, and I do.

Eldora

San Pedro, Salinas Valley, California
Tuesday, November 4, 1851

Dear Cousin Sallie,

Very much has happened since I wrote to tell you of the little boy, Rafael. On Friday morning a woman brought two small girls to the door of the inn. The daughters were so alike that it was hard to find a single difference between them. The woman with them looked much older than my mother, but we soon learned that these were her children, the youngest of many.

"I am Maria," she said, looking first at me and then at my mother, "and here are Isabela and Carmen."

The story she told was much like the story Lucia's mother told except that this woman was not returning to Mexico. She was ill. She was so ill, so weak, she said, she could not take care of the daughters. She had heard that other children, also

Mexicanos, were living at the inn of the kind *señora*. And would the kind *señora*—

My mother interrupted before the question was completed. She kept an inn, she said, not an orphanage.

"Please," the woman said. "I must ask you again. Please—there is no other place."

But my mother had already turned away. Just before she entered her own room—it is halfway between the entry and the door to the garden—she paused, looked back over her shoulder, and told Abdulia she might give the mother and the two girls food. "But food only. They may not, must not, stay. We are already caring for two children—"

"Please," the woman called after her. She was begging now. "I do not ask for myself. But the children—my beautiful children, *señora!*"

My mother made no reply, and in another minute we heard the closing of her door.

Not long afterward I heard my mother giving Alberto instructions about a calf that had been born that morning and some further work that one of the fences required. It was as if nothing had happened.

When Abdulia signaled that our dinner was ready, we found the table perfectly set, which was also as if nothing had happened, with a small vase of flowers between my place and my mother's. But Abdulia did not smile when she brought our food from the kitchen, and when she set it down before us, I found I was not hungry. We ate in silence, and the only reason I ate at all was because I did not want to hurt Abdulia's feelings.

It was the same at the evening meal.

The next morning, which was Saturday, our breakfast was not waiting, the tortillas were already cold, and Abdulia was not to be seen.

Alberto told us that Abdulia had learned where the *muchachas* lived. It was a nearby village, he said, and Abdulia had gone to find someone who would care for the little girls until the mother was healthy. "And if there is no one?" my mother asked. Then, Alberto told us, she meant to take Isabela and Carmen into her own home, where Rafael already sleeps. "It is more important," she had told Alberto, "to care for children when their mother is ill than to prepare meals for rich travelers."

"Abdulia is not the only cook in the valley," my

mother said. "And this will not be the first time I have eaten cold tortillas."

Some thing inside me snapped.

"This is not about cold tortillas!" I said, perhaps too loudly. "It is about you refusing to allow two children whose mother is ill to stay at the *posada*. It is about our having so much food that last night we could not finish what was served to us. It is about us—and the children of other people! It is about Abdulia, who has so much less than we do, who has gone to help!"

My mother continued eating for several minutes. Then, speaking quietly, distinctly, and slowly, as she does when talking to persons who may not understand, she gave her answer.

"It is as I have told you, Eldora. I keep an inn, not an orphanage. I have done what I can, permitted what is possible, for Lucia and Rafael. But I cannot be charitable to all who are in need. If I were to take these girls, that would not be the end of it, Eldora, but only the beginning. More would come, and more. It is not as simple as you would like to think."

"You do not know what I think, and you do not care," I retorted.

My mother did not trouble to answer me. I watched as she pushed her chair back from the table, stood up, and smoothed her dress.

"As it happens, I am quite busy this morning," she said. "And so, if you will excuse me, Eldora . . ."

Watching her, knowing that later I might not have the courage to say what was now on my mind, I caught her hand and began to speak before she could direct me to be silent.

"Only suppose," I said, "that Aunt and Uncle had refused to take *me* in when Captain Shipman . . ." But I could not complete the thought, and my mother removed her hand from mine and told me that my agitation was unfortunate and that I needed to calm myself.

It is so different from what I imagined when I chose to leave Aunt and Uncle and San Francisco and to come to my mother and San Pedro!

I feel very alone here. Not lonely, but *alone.*

Now more than ever, I wish you were here.

Eldora

San Pedro, Salinas Valley, California
Wednesday, November 19, 1851

Dear Cousin Sallie,

After I wrote to you about what has happened here,
and knowing it would be several months at best
before I might hear from you, I wrote to Aunt. My
letter told of the difficulties that have arisen and
pleaded for her help. I considered destroying the
letter as soon as I finished writing it, and perhaps I
should have done so. Rather sooner than I expected,
I received Aunt's reply.

Yes, she understood that I was "deeply troubled."
But no, she could not be of help. I had chosen to
make my life with my mother. If, in consequence, I
came upon hard times as well as happiness, that
was to be expected. I would have to find my own way.
That sounded so like Aunt I could almost hear her
voice when I read it.

At the end of the letter Aunt wrote of her "great

hope and confidence" that, however hard the lesson, the learning would be worthwhile.

Truth to tell, I do not see what there is to learn from this except that Rafael, Isabela, and Carmen are made homeless by my mother's indisposition. As for Lucia, I do not dare to think what awaits her if my mother decides she cannot stay.

Most troubling of all is that my mother sees her refusal to help Rafael and the others as a matter of necessity, nothing more.

If you hear of any one intending to remove to California because California is golden, tell them it is not so.

Eldora

San Pedro, Salinas Valley, California
Monday, December 1, 1851

Dear Aunt,

I have read your letter many times. At first I was disappointed that although you reminded me quite sternly of the sugar and salt of life—how many times have I heard that expression!—you declined to instruct me further. It was only gradually that I recognized that your counsel served me better than advice might have done. Nor is this the first such occasion. How often in the past have you, and Uncle as well, encouraged me in my own efforts, and the results have been all the sweeter.

I believe I have gotten my temper in hand and my thoughts in order. And so, with this letter, I wish to tell of some thing that will, I think, please you, and Uncle, too. I have become a teacher to the four small children—Lucia, whom you know, and Rafael, Isabela, and Carmen—of whom I have written and who are still here, at least in the daytime, despite my mother's harsh words.

If Uncle will send just one book for my little scholars, I would be so happy to have it. I think it will please them to see, in a *book*, the words they have been spelling with letters inscribed, with charcoal, on their hands! They are very clever, these children, and eager to learn. I have made up a very short story about Cat and Rat! The story is: "One day CAT and RAT were SAD and MAD. So they RAN away."

If someone makes a mistake, and turns "cat" into "hat," we all laugh about it together.

My schoolroom is the back half of the porch. Alberto, whom you may remember, as he was the driver when my mother and I and Luke and his father came to San Francisco, has made some small benches for the little ones and a table for me.

The next time my mother goes to San Francisco, I hope I may go with her. When we were there before, we were all thinking about Luke's father and praying for a safe voyage, and there was no time when we could talk.

Has Luke received a letter from his Pa as he

calls him? It is nearly two months since Mr. Hall left California, and perhaps he will have written from Panama City or even Chagres. I wonder how far he has gotten and I hope he has enjoyed a smooth voyage.

I hope you are well. I miss the corrugated castle, it having been our first home in California, and I wish I could see you and Uncle and Luke, too. But I think I said that already.

I am, as ever,
Your Eldora

San Pedro, Salinas Valley, California
Friday, December 5, 1851

Dear Cousin Sallie,

Some thing so strange and sweet and sad happened today that I must tell you at once (even if all I am able to do is set it down on paper and know that many weeks will pass before you receive it).

I was sitting outside with Lucia, who held, as she often does, her well-loved, ragged doll. I noticed that she was looking angry—which is unusual for Lucia—but could not discover the cause. All at once, and without saying any thing, she threw the doll into the road.

"I have too much trouble with you," she told the doll. "That is why I am throwing you away and leaving you here. Soon I will get a new doll."

"But Lucia," I said, collecting the unfortunate doll from where it lay in the dust, "she is your doll since a long, long time ago. I think you will be sorry if you do not have her anymore."

Lucia looked at me defiantly. "No," she said. "No. I will not be sorry, and my mother, who has left me here, she is not sorry either."

"Oh, Lucia!" I said, putting my arms around her. "Oh, Lucia! I think that is not so."

I almost said, "Look at me, Lucia! My mother sent me away. But now I am here with her!"

But instead of saying that, I told Lucia a story. I put my name in it, but it was her story too. While I was telling it, Lucia reached out and took back the doll—which I had been keeping on my lap—and cradled it.

When I came to the end of my story, she looked up at me and said, "I think this doll does not like to be a no-name doll anymore. Now I will call her Eldora."

"And I will like that," I said, "very, very much."

A few minutes later Fernanda called, and we went inside. I was holding Lucia's left hand, and she—with the right—held my new namesake.

I hope you do not find my story too foolish. I have recalled it as well as I can and set it down for you. I enclose it here.

Eldora

Once upon a time there was a little girl, and her name was Eldora. Her mother was very, very sick. She was so sick she could not sleep, and it hurt her ears if her little girl cried or made noise. She was so sick she could not take care of her little girl.

One day the little girl asked her mother to play with her. Her mother said, "I am too sick to play with you. You must play by yourself, Eldora."

The next day the little girl asked her mother for some thing to eat. The mother said, "I am too sick to cook your food. Others will cook for you and give you food."

On the third day the little girl asked her mother to tell her a story. The mother said, "I am too sick to tell stories. You will have to make up your own story or tell yourself a story you have heard before."

On the fourth day a sea captain came to visit. "My ship is ready to sail," he said to the mother. "Will you come with me?"

The mother said, "I am too sick to sail with you on your ship. But if you take my daughter on your ship, you will see that she can play by herself, she can eat food that others cook, and she can tell herself a story. These things, and more, my daughter can do. And when the voyage comes to an end, she will stay where you live and be happy."

"I will do as you ask," said the captain.

"And one thing more," the mother said. "Please tell my daughter three times every day that even though I am far away, I will love her forever and ever. And tell her also that I promise that one day, some day, she will see me again."

San Pedro, Salinas Valley, California
Saturday, December 13, 1851

Dear Cousin Sallie,

When Lucia thrust her doll into the road and I told
the story I made up, I did not think that any one
was near or that it would have mattered. After all,
it was only a simple tale, made up to save a well-
loved doll from a dusty death. A day or so later, my
mother told me that she had, in fact, been standing
near the window that opens onto my schoolroom.
She had seen Lucia throw her doll into the road and
overheard our conversation. I at once wondered if
I was about to be reprimanded for enrolling myself
in the rescue of Lucia's doll. But it was my story
she wanted to talk about. She had been thinking
about it, and there was some thing she wanted to
ask me.

"I wonder," she began, "that we have not spoken
of it before. But I suppose we each had our reasons.

"Not many days ago," she went on, "you asked me to consider what might have happened had Captain Shipman's aunt and uncle not taken you into their home.

"What do you suppose would have happened, you challenged me, had they not done this? And now I must ask, why do you suppose I gave you to Captain Shipman and asked that he take you to your father?"

"Because you were sick," I said, "and when I cried, you could not sleep."

"Oh, my dear Eldora!" my mother cried out. "Did you really think that was the reason?"

I nodded.

"And that was all?"

I nodded again.

"And did you not think then, or thereafter, how it would have been if I *had* died, and you—a child not yet three years old—had been left alone in Panama City with no one to look after you? No one, even, who knew you and could take you to your father who was, I believed, awaiting us in Buena Vista. That, if you remember, was all I asked of Captain Shipman."

I could not reply because I had never thought of these things. I just believed that my mother was a beautiful lady, a princess, a queen! And when she fell ill, I had been a trouble to her. So she had tossed me aside as Lucia had done with her doll.

Then a new thought struck me.

"Aunt never told me the rest of the story," I said, "about my father that was to meet the ship, but he was dead, and then Captain Shipman took me to her and Uncle. Did she know?" I asked.

"I think she knew," my mother said softly. "But perhaps she believed that telling you these things would only make you sad. Or perhaps she told you some thing of the sort, some thing that you—being such a little girl—could not understand, and so you did not remember."

"No," I insisted. "She did not tell me and I did not know."

"But now you do," my mother said. "Some times, no matter how hard we try, we simply cannot imagine what a little child might think. And we make mistakes."

I turned to my mother and put my arms around her, burying my face as I did so in the soft silk of her dress. "All the time—all this time—I thought you sent me away because I cried and . . ."

"It was a pestilent city," my mother said, stroking my hair as she spoke, "and I feared, and others feared, that I would not live. It was to save you, Eldora, so that you would not become ill or be left alone in a country of strangers. Only for that. Only and solely for that. Not for all the sleep in the world would I have sent you away."

When I looked up, my mother's eyes were filled with tears. And so were mine.

With my mother holding me, I wept for minutes on end. When I was able to stop, and could sniff the last of the tears away, my mother held out a handkerchief.

"Trick," she said, and each of us managed a smile remembering the first trip from San Francisco to San Pedro and how, on that occasion, she had cheered me with her trick when I cried.

I do not know if any one was watching us. But now, with my mother leading me as carefully as if I were a little child, we walked—without speaking— all the way to the very end of the garden and all the way back.

"How little we know," my mother said thoughtfully, "and to think that I, a grown woman, was as ignorant of your thoughts and fears as you were of my reasons."

More silence. Then, in a voice that seemed to change the subject but in truth did not, she said, "The children cannot stay here, as you know. But some place is needed. And I will think on it."

"So will I," I said, not knowing quite what I meant. But I think my mother understood, and that was all that mattered.

My heart is full to bursting.

I will write soon again and am

Yours, as ever,
Eldora

CHAPTER VII

Eldora

JANUARY 12, 1852 – MAY 3, 1852

Even as no story begins of itself,
so may a story remain incomplete
although it has reached the end.

JOHN HALL, TRAVELS IN THE WEST

San Pedro, Salinas Valley, California
Monday, January 12, 1852

Dear Cousin Sallie,

After that tearstained walk in the garden my mother made only a few short trips and was not away very long. We spent more time together than usual, and I think both of us enjoyed it. One day my mother told me stories about when she was a girl. Another time she described, room by room, the house she and my father had when they were first married. Over our meals together, with no guests present, she talked about books she had encouraged me to read, and the books became much more interesting! (Once I nearly forgot to eat for listening to her tell that when she was about my age, she had secretly enjoyed writing poems.)

Best of all was the day she showed me a tiny silk dress with blue embroidery that had been mine when I was less than two years old! Among several that she had sewn for me, it was her favorite, and she had taken it with her. It was the keepsake she meant to show my father when he met us in California. But, she said, it seemed too sentimental an errand to ask of Captain Shipman, and so she had kept the dress. She told me that she had never shown it to any one, not even Señor Ramos, and wondered aloud if, somehow, she had always believed that one day she would show it to me.

As you can imagine, I loved hearing about these things and thought my mother would always find new stories to tell, and then I would no longer be such a lonely princess.

Foolish me!

I ought to have remembered, having been here last year at this time, that in this part of California the celebration of Christmas begins twelve days *before* Christmas, which is the first day of Advent, and goes on until twelve days *after* Christmas. During this whole time every house is decorated with poinsettias—beautiful plants with red flowers and pointed leaves. The *posada* is no different in this regard. There was even a small poinsettia in my mother's room and one in mine also.

Processions wind through the streets, and there are long church services and *piñatas*, which are special games for the children that end with showers of small treats. Never mind that there are not many children in San Pedro! Nieces and nephews come from nearby villages (where they have probably had their own celebrations), and it is a happy time.

January 6th, when it all comes to an end, is called *Día de los Reyes*, which means "Day of the Kings." It celebrates the coming of the three kings to see the baby in the manger.

January 6th was six days ago.

This morning a messenger arrived. Please, he asked, could the *señora* come with him? He had come to tell of a bad dispute between a miner with a hot temper and an individual he accused of being a claim jumper. When the hot-tempered miner drew his knife, the claim jumper showed his gun. "First I will kill you," he said, "and then . . . your friends!"

So someone said what they always say, "Let us send for the *señora*, she will know what to do!" Every one was happy when the men agreed to put away their weapons, but only, they said, until the *señora* is arrived.

Believing that she had no choice, my mother quickly readied herself for a hasty leave-taking.

The distance to be traveled was not great, and she chose to ride, using her favorite horse. Alberto said she was taking a needless risk, but my mother insisted and the horse was fetched from the pasture. She greeted the animal fondly, told me she was sorry she had to leave so suddenly, and gave instructions to Fernanda and Abdulia (who hardly needed them). She mounted with her usual grace, and then she was gone.

I was sorely disappointed, for I had persuaded myself that things were now going to be different. And because I connected this with our long walk in the garden, I had not considered that the miners and *rancheros* had been too much occupied with celebrating Christmas to engage in the usual disputes. Therefore, they had not required my mother's attention. That was why my mother had stayed in San Pedro and, also because of the holiday celebrations, there had been no travelers staying at the *posada*. My mother was therefore able to spend time with me. It had nothing to do with the thoughts and feelings that we had exchanged. It had nothing to do with me.

The next day

I had not completed this letter when the mother of Carmen and Isabela, escorted by her daughters, appeared at the door. The mother explained that she had hoped to see the *señora*, but—perhaps—she could speak with me instead. That, as you may imagine, put an end to my letter writing.

The mother, being no longer sick and as strong as ever, had come to fetch the daughters. She was so happy to see them and, plain to see, they were happy too.

Blinking away my tears because the mother of Carmen and Isabela had come to fetch *them*, whereas *my* mother had just left *me*, I heard myself say, "Oh, but they are such good students!" This was beside the point at that moment, but it was the first thing that came to mind.

"*Sí*," she said, smiling at my compliment to her daughters. Then she thanked me very much that they had been able to attend *la escuela de la señorita* and had been so well cared for. "But," she said, "now that I am well, the best place for my daughters is with *su mamá*, with me."

The daughters smiled to hear these words, and Carmen, who is the bolder of the two, asked if they might take their pencils with them—a remembrance of the *escuela*, and of me.

I nodded, "yes," and thus encouraged she asked if they might have some paper as well! *No one will need it now,* I thought, and I presented to each of them several sheets of paper.

Then all that remained was to say good-bye, which we did, and also *adiós*. Then we said *adiós* and good-bye several times more—and when they left, my little *escuela* was smaller by half.

I have heard that Rafael's mother intends to come for *him*. If that is so, my school will have no purpose. Nor will I, in being here.

And Lucia, you will ask? It is true that she shares my room. But I think she is happier with Fernanda and is no longer so interested in reading, or improving her handwriting, or doing sums.

Abdulia is calling me to dinner, so I must put my letter writing aside. When my mother is away, I take my meals with her, Fernanda, Lucia, and Alberto. Abdulia likes us to come promptly when she calls, and I have learned that it is not good to vex Abdulia. When my mother is here—and there are guests—Abdulia is much more willing to wait.

I am most surely

Yours, as ever,
Eldora

San Pedro, Salinas Valley, California
Tuesday, January 27, 1852

Dear Cousin Sallie,

I have had a letter from Luke in which he writes that he is working for the man who bought Mr. Lewisohn's store, and that Uncle, using a space once occupied by a store, has enrolled several new scholars—girls as well as boys—and there are now thirteen altogether. If I were in San Francisco, Uncle would have fourteen scholars!

Among the newly enrolled scholars is a Chinese girl. Her name Po-lai Wu. She is one year too young to be in the same class as Luke, so she and I are the same age and maybe I will be friends with her. Her parents maintain a restaurant that is said to be excellent.

Some weeks ago I told my mother that I thought I was falling behind in my schoolwork because of doing my lessons by myself. She replied that many people would be pleased to have lessons that are prepared especially for them. But, she said, she has heard of a school for "young women" in Monterey. Perhaps that would please me more?

"No," I said. "The main reason I came here is to make my home with you! It would hardly serve that purpose to remove to Monterey to attend school there!"

This clearly pleased my mother, who then admitted that she had her own misgivings about the school in Monterey. When I asked what they might be, she said it seemed that most of the students were the daughters of wealthy persons and that the school prepares them to become the wives of wealthy husbands.

In that case, I said, I certainly did not think it would suit me very well and, laughing at the way I had put it, she agreed. Needless to say, nothing more has been said about the Monterey school. I continue to do the lessons Uncle sends, and my mother corrects them.

Several of my mother's friends have suggested that a tutor might be engaged. But my mother, thinking how often she is called away, has told them that she is not pleased to imagine a stranger, no matter how well educated, living here at the inn. And what would Abdulia and Fernanda say if this stranger was a man!

When my mother visited the corrugated castle and there was no longer any doubt but that I was not an orphan, I thought my life had become a fairy tale! Surely my mother, who even had golden hair, was a fairy-tale mother! When she then suggested that her home be my home, I truly thought that my every wish had come true! (I realized later that *Mi casa es su casa* is a common saying here and one she uses often.)

We were all so proud, Aunt and Uncle and I, that my mother had kept and even enlarged her husband's properties! On that occasion neither I nor any one else remembered that inns and ranches and mines require the attention of their owners. No one noted that San Pedro had no school. No one considered that a *Mexicano* village might not offer friends. No one asked what I was to do when my mother had to be away, seeing to business matters, nor did I. I was so happy that my mother was alive and that I was not an orphan, such questions were far from my mind.

272

=

VII. ELDORA

They are now the very questions that I ask myself, and some times I wonder if, after all, I should not have left San Francisco.

I hope my next letter will strike a happier note and that you will not think unkindly of me,

Your most faithful,
Eldora

San Pedro, Salinas Valley, California
Thursday, February 5, 1852

Dear Cousin Sallie,

Lucia put forward an odd request this morning. She wanted, she said, to go to Fernanda's house to see the newborn baby goat that Fernanda told her about.

"But Lucia," I said. "Alberto has many goats right here! Big ones, small ones—whatever size you like, he has them all!"

"*Sí,*" she said. "But Fernanda's goats are in the yard of her house, so I can see them better."

When she said that, I remembered a letter from Luke in which he told of a picture Miguel had drawn for Lucia. It was about their mother's house, and in the yard there were chickens and a cat and a pig. And a goat! Fernanda's goats must remind Lucia of the goat in her mother's yard, and perhaps Fernanda's adobe resembles her mother's house and reminds her of her mother. And that, I realized, was the reason Lucia preferred Fernanda's goats to the goats of the *señora*.

Patiently, as is her way, Lucia stood waiting for my answer. But instead of replying to her at once, I found myself remembering the corrugated castle and the yard, where Aunt and I made and sold our pies. In my mind's eye Aunt stood in the doorway, and she was smiling and calling my name.

It seemed so real I had almost turned to answer her when a tug on my hand reminded me that it was Lucia, and not Aunt, who was calling me.

Yes, I told Lucia, she might go with Fernanda. And then, sounding exactly like Aunt, I said that she must not stay too long or be a nuisance to Fernanda.

By that time Fernanda had reached the street, and Lucia had to hurry to catch up with her.

That night I dreamed about Aunt.

In my dream we were selling pies, and Aunt sent me to fetch the sign—the one I made, Luke says they still use. But I could not find the sign, although I searched for it. I was troubled when I woke up, and in fact, for this entire day I have been cross and ill humored.

Once, when I was in a pout, my mother said that girls my age are often inclined to be moody.

I do not feel either poutish or moody today. But if any one were to ask me whatever is the matter, I would not know what to say.

I am yours, as ever,
Eldora

San Pedro, Salinas Valley, California
Monday, February 23, 1852

Dear Cousin Sallie,

Shortly after I wrote to you about Lucia and the newborn goat, we went to Monterey. Some matters required my mother's attention, which often happens, so on this occasion I was surprised when she proposed that I travel with her. She thought I had seemed quite down-hearted of late and that a "change of scene" might help.

Several of the people we met in Monterey asked after "the newspaper writer from Michigan," so he must have made a good impression. We were pleased to tell them that, having crossed the isthmus safely, Mr. Hall had written from Chagres and was in excellent health.

On the second day we were there we paid a visit to my mother's dressmaker. The clothes I brought from San Francisco are now quite outgrown, and even the cornflower blue silk and several other dresses made since I came have become too short and too snug, especially the bodice.

For "every day" I selected a full-skirted, but otherwise simple dress. It is to be made in a dark green plaid. For fiestas we chose a more elaborate style, to be made in purple silk. The color reminds me of Luke's purple shirt, and I said so. But the dressmaker and my mother prefer to call it "wine colored" and speak of it as "very fashionable."

My two dresses, and several my mother ordered for herself, will be ready for fitting the next time we are in Monterey.

Because we were to attend a performance at the theater, I had asked my mother if we might take the amethyst earrings, and that night I wore them.

Usually I do not tell any one how the earrings came to be mine, but after the performance our host's youngest daughter admired them, and I told their story. She said it was the most romantic thing she had ever heard.

We returned to the *posada* on Friday. It felt good to be back in San Pedro, and we were fondly welcomed by Lucia, Abdulia, and Fernanda. Lucia had even copied a WELCOME HOME message from one of the books I had read with her and placed it in my room. As you may imagine, that pleased me very much.

When I asked Abdulia about Rafael, who was nowhere to be seen, she said that "someone"—she did not think it was his mother—had come for him. Abdulia said he cried when he was told that he could not stay at the *posada* any longer, and the lady led him away. I feel so sorry for that quiet little boy. He had just begun to tease and laugh and play. I wish I had been here to tell him good-bye.

That evening my mother, who had not mentioned it before, told me that she had spoken with several of her friends about the "plight of valley children." Although they agreed, one by one, that it was a sad and difficult matter, no one offered assistance or had a suggestion to make. She found this disappointing.

I had hoped to find a letter from you, but none awaited. I will be happy to have news of you and am

Yours, as always,
Eldora

San Pedro, Salinas Valley, California
Friday, March 12, 1852

Dear Cousin Sallie,

I think I have told you that I am making a small cushion with an embroidered cover for my mother. It has a patterned border, and I have decided to place a design of wild mustard—both the leaves and the flowers—in the center. The first time I saw wild mustard was in San Francisco. Uncle says it does not grow in places like Vermont or New Hampshire, so probably it does not grow in Massachusetts, either. (This would explain why I had not seen it before, and probably you have not seen it.) The next time I saw it was on the trip from San Francisco to San Pedro. I can hardly think of it as a weed, which it is, as the flowers are so beautiful—a deep and beautiful yellow that glows more brightly than gold.

In the space below the flowers I will work *Mi casa es su casa* and then the date. Abdulia helped me draw the flowers, and Fernanda helped me plan out the writing. It is to be worked in blue, my mother's favorite color, and as Fernanda rightly observed, it sets off the green leaves and golden flowers. As you can see, Abdulia and Fernanda have been very helpful.

This morning, directly after breakfast, I took my sewing box and seated myself out of doors. I like to watch the people passing by, although, to be truthful, San Pedro is a very small village and there are very few people except on market days. Usually they walk and are barefoot. But if they are bringing things home or taking them to market, they will be using their *carretas*. The *rancheros*, who some times ride right through the middle of town and do not care that they are throwing up a great deal of dust, will be handsomely dressed.

This morning, after smoothing and straightening all I had accomplished, I threaded my needle and began to work. The sun was warm, but not too warm, and people waved at me as they walked by—even Señor Espinosa, who is cross with most people but took a liking to Luke. I returned his greeting.

Perhaps it was because I was not paying close attention to my work that a kink came into the thread I was using, which then frayed and broke. I had no choice but to take out the broken thread all the way back to where I had started it. Doing this one stitch at a time is a tedious task, as you know. So I was glad to be nearly done with it when the needle slipped, split a second thread, and thereby doubled the damage.

I should have put my unfortunate work away! Instead, I persisted and consequently pricked my finger so badly I had no choice but to put the work away lest my bleeding finger stain the cloth.

When Fernanda came by a few minutes later, she found me with my work in my lap, my finger in my mouth (hoping to stop the bleeding thereby), and very close to tears.

Others might have paid no mind. But Fernanda kneeled down close to my chair and called me her *pobrecita*, her poor little *señorita*, and wished to know what had happened.

Without giving an answer, I showed her my needlework and pointed out the mistakes. Meaning to cheer me, Fernanda made light of the damage. It is not a problem, she said, *no problema*, and the work could be easily fixed.

"Yes," I said, "but I am also sad for other things that are not so easily fixed. I have no friends here, and my mother is too often away. Also, the children of my little school are gone, all except Lucia, Abdulia thinks I am clumsy with my sewing, Alberto preferred Luke, who is not here anyway, and even the cover for my mother's pillow . . ."

Fernanda listened patiently. But, alas for Fernanda, when I paused to collect my thoughts, she said what they always say: "*La señora* will know what to do."

"No she will not!" I flung at her. "Because there are things *la señora* does *not* know how to do."

"Oh, *señorita*," said Fernanda. "*Tu madre—*"

But I rushed on. "My mother does not know how to tell me about my father, and she does not know that I need to go to a school, a real school, and she does not care that here in San Pedro I am not needed by any one, and no one would miss me if I was gone, and I think that perhaps I should not be here at all."

I surprised myself with saying that aloud and, as I was not able to go on, looked to Fernanda for help.

"I think," she said, rising to her feet, "that you

have said too much to me and not enough to *tu madre*. Always it is *importante* to tell the correct person. If you show the broken thread to me, I— Fernanda—cannot help you because I myself do not do sewing very well. But if you ask Abdulia, who makes such beautiful things, Abdulia will help you.

"So," she said, "when *tu madre* is here, you must say to her what you have said to me, because she is the correct person. And if you do not tell her, if you hide it like the sewing in your lap, then I, Fernanda, will tell her, because she loves you very much."

I had never heard Fernanda say so much at one time, and much of it was in Spanish, which I have not tried to write down because you would not understand it.

Abdulia was busy at the stove when we surprised her by arriving in her kitchen. But when Fernanda explained the difficulty, Abdulia set down the wooden spoon with which she was stirring the sauce, and when I showed her what had happened to my needlework, she understood at once. Then she showed me how I ought to hold the needle and watched me until I had gotten it right. I think Abdulia was pleased that I asked for her help.

Fernanda stayed in the kitchen while all this was happening. Then, seeing that Abdulia had known what to do and that I did not need her any longer, she signaled that she must return to her work.

"But," she said, pausing at the door, "you must remember that when *tu madre* returns to the *posada*, you must tell her all that you told me. Because if you do not tell her—"

"I know," I said, "then you will do it yourself. But I think that will not be necessary. Besides," I added, surprised that I was able to smile, "I think I will do it better."

Please be well and write to me when you can.

Ever yours,
Eldora

San Pedro, Salinas Valley, California
Friday, March 19, 1852

Dear Cousin Sallie,

I told her!

I did not do it the day she returned, because she was tired, and I did not do it the next day because I was too scared. But yesterday morning, because I did not want Fernanda to be the one to tell her—that is when I told her.

Between the kitchen garden and the inn there is a wooden bench and a small table. Some times Fernanda uses it when she is picking over the vege-tables she has selected for Abdulia. Yesterday, when I chanced to look out of my window, I saw that my mother was seated there and that she was alone.

I patted down my hair and smoothed my dress and went outside to wait for my mother to look up from her work. It was only a few minutes before she caught sight of me. "Yes, Eldora?" she said.

"There is some thing I must tell you," I said. "But I do not know where to begin."

"Well," she said in a good-humored way, "perhaps you should start at the end."

I knew that my mother was joking, but that is just what I did.

"I should not have left San Francisco," I said, and my words came in a rush. "Aunt and Uncle said that the choice must be mine. And when I chose San Pedro, I chose the wrong thing."

I could see that my mother was startled. But after all, she is the *señora* and she is used to being told things that she does not expect, and might not want, to hear.

She replied with a question. "Am I to understand that you wish to return to San Francisco?"

"I do not know," I wailed, sounding about the age of Lucia. "I do not know," I repeated. "So I need you to tell me."

"I do not know if I can do that," she said. "Perhaps Mr. and Mrs. Holt? Have you written to them about this?"

"No," I said. "Before I told you, I told only Fernanda."

"What has Fernanda to do with this?" she asked rather sharply.

So I finally told my mother what I had told Fernanda, and maybe a little bit more. She was not angry, as I had feared. Only thoughtful, and perhaps a little sad.

"I am afraid you leave me a bit confused," she said after a pause. "But Fernanda was right about asking the right person. And I do not think you were wrong about choosing San Pedro. And possibly you are right about returning to San Francisco."

I thought she had said two opposite things. But if neither one of them was wrong, did that mean both were right? I was going to ask her, but Alberto came along just then, which ended the conversation.

That night I could not sleep.

I used to think that sleepless nights only happened to other people. Some times Aunt would tell Uncle that she hadn't slept well at all; some times Uncle had a bad night and grumbled in the morning; never had it been me. Now I listened to the ticking of my little mantel clock, one of my mother's extravagant gifts to me, and wondered uselessly if Aunt and Uncle would welcome me back to the corrugated castle. Would they even *have* me back? If they did, where would Luke stay? Would those enrolled at Uncle's school be far advanced in scholarship and learning beyond what I have mastered with my lonely lessons? Would Luke be my friend?

As you can see, my mind is filled with questions. When I have some answers, I will write to you again. In the meantime, I shall be thinking of you and asking myself what you would say if you were nearby. It is not for the first time, nor I imagine the last, that I find myself wishing that you were here, right here, right now.

Eldora

San Pedro, Salinas Valley, California
Wednesday, March 24, 1852

Dear Cousin Sallie,

This morning my mother called me aside and suggested that a walk would "do us good." For a while we spoke about ordinary things—a roof that had recently been replaced, a baby playing in the dust of the road while the mother hung out the clothes she had just washed. I was beginning to wonder why my mother had suggested a walk and what "good" she thought it would do.

I soon found out.

"When you came to San Pedro," she said, talking as if Alberto had not interrupted us on Friday, "we both had much to learn, much, much more than either of us imagined. And quite different, too. And learning those things *would* never, indeed *could* never, have taken place had you not dared to leave San Francisco to make your home with me."

When I said that I did not understand, she began again.

"Had you not come to San Pedro," she said, "you might well have continued to believe that I was the fairy-tale queen you had always imagined. And," she continued, "until I saw how sad and troubled you looked when I left on my trips, until the day you raged at me about the children I could not take in, if such things, and others, had never come to pass, I might have permitted myself to suppose that I could simply include you in my life without changing it one iota."

"Iota," I said. "What is that?"

"That is a word that started out as Greek and means 'one little bit.'"

"Iota," I repeated. "I think 'iota' is a good word to know. And perhaps the truth of the matter is that I do not wish you to change yourself or your life—not by one iota. Besides," I added, "who would take the place of the *señora*, on whom every one depends?"

My mother laughed when I said this, and I did too. It was as if a morning fog had lifted, a San Francisco morning fog, and the sun came out.

That night I did not readily fall asleep, which

is different from being sleepless. I was happy and grateful that my mother did not think I had been wrong when I chose San Pedro. It was just that what I found proved to be quite the opposite of what I had expected.

When I had got that clearly in mind, I knew that I could tell my mother that it made me happy that the *posada* had become my home, that Fernanda and Abdulia were dearer than dear to me, that I admired Alberto (and I knew that Luke did too). I now could say that I loved her very much and was proud to be her daughter. And I knew that when those things had been said, I would be free to leave.

Eldora

San Pedro, Salinas Valley, California
Friday, April 16, 1852

Dear Cousin Sallie,

For the first time in my life I woke up on the sixteenth day of April and knew that this day, and no other, was exactly the day on which I was born. When Aunt would be writing important days in the family Bible, I used to ask, "But when was *I* born?"

"Oh, Eldora," she would say. "That is some thing we cannot know. Only that we are glad that you were born and came to live with us."

"But Aunt," I would say. "Every one has a birthday! And there you have written them down— 'Cassie,' 'Asa,' and 'Willie,' for the children of your sister, and after Cassie's birth date, the day on which she died. And the same for Henry, who was your little boy with Uncle. . . ."

But I would see that I was making her sad. So then I would ask her to show me the day on which she and Uncle had gotten married, and she would point to "Sunday, September 25, 1831." So now, if she wished to do so, she could very carefully write "April 16, 1837" for the day that I was born.

When we sat down to breakfast this morning, I noted a book, finely bound, beside my mother's plate. But she did not mention it, and therefore neither did I.

We were nearly done with our meal when my mother said she supposed that I knew why the day was special. "My birthday?" I allowed.

"Yes," she said, "your birthday."

Then she lifted the little book and passed it over to me. After I read the title aloud, *The Sonnets of William Shakespeare*, she suggested that I turn to the flyleaf. There, in an unfamiliar hand, it was written: "To my daughter, Eldora, on her birthday. May she enjoy a long and happy life, confident of the enduring affection of her devoted father." Below that was the date: April 16, 1838.

"But I thought I was born in 1837—"

My mother interrupted before my sentence was complete. "Yes," she said, "that is certainly true. But he gave you this gift on your first birthday, which of course was one year later."

I could not speak, but took her hand, outstretched on the table, and then—on an impulse—I got up and hugged her.

There could be no better time, I thought, for me to give her the present on which I had worked so long.

To my mother's evident surprise, I asked to be excused. Several minutes later I returned to the table and gave my needlework to her. I explained that I had meant to wait until it was completed. But I wished her to have it now, and I hoped she would understand.

I watched as she ran a finger over the bright blue letters.

"'*Mi casa es su casa*,'" she read aloud, her clear voice making the words sound beautiful and grand.

"I wonder," she said, "if you can possibly know what this means to me. And about wild mustard . . ."

"I copied the flowers from the design on my desk," I admitted. "And Abdulia helped me. We both hoped you would like it."

"Well, that is not exactly what I meant," she said. "Rather, has any one told you the story of wild mustard, which is also the story of Father Serra? He was a Franciscan and he came with the intention of establishing missions in the new land. This was a bit more than a hundred years ago, and it is said that he brought with him the seeds of wild mustard."

"Why would he do so?" I asked.

"I think," she said, "it had been his thought that if those seeds rooted, and grew and bloomed, then, when he meant to return to Spain, a golden pathway—a pathway of wild mustard—would lead him to the sheltered bay where his ship awaited.

"I've always liked that story," she said, "perhaps having come from afar myself. So it gives me special pleasure, this gift you have made for me. But now, birthday or no, and the giving of gifts aside, there is work that must be done and we must attend to it."

No sooner had she said this than Abdulia entered the room and began to clear the table of the dishes we had used. It was quite apparent that she had been watching us and I am glad to say she did not scold me later for presenting my gift too soon!

It seemed a good time to tell her that I thought I would not remain in San Pedro much longer and that I would return to San Francisco where I had lived before.

"*Si,*" she said, in a very comfortable voice.

"And this does not surprise you?" I asked.

"No," she said, "because Fernanda has already told me how you are not happy here."

I should have guessed that this might be the case, but no, I had engaged myself in worrying what I would say, and when, and now it was all not necessary! And why should I have guessed that this might be the case? Because here at the *posada* there is no keeping of secrets.

Even though we did not linger over it, it is very nice to have a birthday. And telling Abdulia that I would be leaving soon, which she had *not* been told already, was part of my celebration!

Eldora

San Pedro, Salinas Valley, California
Saturday, April 24, 1852

Dear Cousin Sallie,

Several days after my birthday my mother said that the time had come to write to Aunt and Uncle about my wish to return to San Francisco and to them. She suggested that each of us write our letters privately, and then we might each wish to read one another's letter before we posted them. This surprised me so greatly that I simply stared at her, not knowing what to say. (Aunt would have asked if the cat had got my tongue! But my mother said no such thing, nor did she demand an answer.) In fact, that is what we did, and so I am able to tell you that her letter was clear and logical, whereas mine was rather jumbled.

Much of what my letter contained I have already written to you, so I will not repeat it here. Toward the end of her letter my mother suggested that even if it meant my absence from school, even if it proved to be somewhat inconvenient, she hoped that it might be agreed that every year I would spend the week of my birthday with her in San Pedro.

I wonder if our exchange of gifts suggested this proposal. I cannot tell you how happy I was when I read those words.

Our letters have now been posted, and we await a reply. (When I said some thing of the sort, my mother said she rather thought that there would be a reply from Aunt and another one from Uncle; in other words, two replies.). I then explained that I was really quite certain that there would be but a single reply, and it would be written by Aunt.

Dear Aunt! She and Uncle talk about many things. But if there is a difficult letter to write, Aunt will do the writing.

My mother laughed when I said this. "Octavio wrote our letters," she said, "but as I recall, your father always left the difficult letters to me."

So that is one more thing I know about my father.

We are agreed, my mother and I, that my "transfer" (as she calls it) should not be delayed once it has been decided. I agreed, but did not trouble to tell her that I had already told Abdulia and I rather thought Abdulia had told Fernanda.

With greatest affection,
Eldora

San Pedro, Salinas Valley, California
Monday, May 3, 1852

Dear Cousin Sallie,

The reply from Uncle and Aunt has come—and I was right. They talked at length about my wish to return to San Francisco, and Aunt wrote the letter. She began by saying that even as they had welcomed me to their home when Captain Shipman brought me to New Bedford, they would welcome me now.

"Well," said my mother, "I believe that settles the matter. It will take some getting used to, I allow. But it is good to be assured that they, and we, agree."

When I asked how would we know when I ought to leave, she said that she thought I might stay here until the end of this month and leave on the first of June.

"Convenient and tidy," she said.

Convenient and tidy it surely is, but hearing those words, with their definite sound, made me both happy and sad. If it ever comes about that you are obliged to make a choice such as mine, do not think that all the good lies on one side.

I ought to have learned this lesson when I came to San Pedro. But now I am to leave San Pedro, and the happy and the sad are once more mixed together and it is not so simple to say my good-byes.

One thing that has troubled me very much has come to a happy ending. It is, or rather *was*, about Lucia. Would she remain at the *posada* after I leave? Who, in my stead, would praise her when praise is deserved and reprimand her for errors?

When I told my worries to Fernanda she said, "Oh but *señorita*, it is not so *difícil*! Lucia will make her home with me, and I will be glad for that. She already knows the way, the newest of the goats comes to her when she calls, and when you visit the *señora*, as you will surely do, Lucia will show you every new thing she has learned."

"And Lucia's mother?" I asked. "Do you think that one day she will come to San Pedro and—"

"*Quién sabe,*" Fernanda said. "*Quién sabe.* But it is certain that Lucia will be here and if her mother comes here, here she will find Lucia."

As it happened, two days later when Fernanda

and I were talking, Lucia asked my permission to visit Fernanda's goats.

"Yes," I said, "You may do that. But first there is something we must talk about."

"*¿Mi madre?*" she asked eagerly.

I did not know how to answer her question, but to Fernanda it was clear that before Lucia found out in some other way, I—the *señorita*—must tell Lucia that I mean to leave San Pedro.

So that is when, more plainly and simply than I had thought possible, I told Lucia that when I left San Pedro, I would return to San Francisco, and the corrugated castle.

"With Aunt and Uncle?" Lucia asked.

"With Aunt and Uncle," I said.

It took Lucia less than a moment to consider this information.

"I think *they* will be happy," she told me solemnly, "and I think *you* will be happy. But for me it is sad."

"Yes," said Fernanda, "but some times it is good to be sad which is a true feeling. And I think you will come to me in my *adobe* and you will help me in my garden, and we will make one another happy, and also Esperanza!"

Lucia recognized the joke and echoed its final words. *"Si,"* she said, "especially Esperanza."

"So now we can smile again," Fernanda said. "And you, Eldora, must promise that when you will visit the *señora*, you will also visit Lucia and me and Esperanza—"

"—and Abdulia and Alberto," Lucia said, "because they are my San Pedro family too!"

Fernanda and I fell silent, but Lucia, having made this important observation, turned to another matter.

"And now," she said, "may I go with Fernanda to her *casa* because the goats will like to see me?"

"Yes," I said, "now you may go with Fernanda."

At that, Lucia put her arms around my waist and hugged me hard. Whether it was to thank me for permitting her to go with Fernanda, or to tell me that she loved me, I do not know. Quite possibly it was for both reasons. We shared a happy moment.

"And," said Fernanda as if she was telling us what she had been thinking, "when the time comes that you, Eldora, leave the *posada*, and Lucia is sad, I will say to her that I love her and I will take care of her as long as it is needed."

Fernanda's promise, which I have repeated to myself several times, has made me much more peaceful.

I was glad to hear that you and Billy Winslow have become good friends, he having long since forgiven you for being better at spelling! As you know, Luke and I did not like each other at first, but that changed when he was here. Now we write quite often to each other, although not as often as I write to you.

Luke likes to joke about all the practice he got writing letters for the miners when he was at Roaring Springs. Lest you are inclined to wonder, be it ever so slightly, the letters that he writes to me are not in the least like the love notes that he wrote for the miners, nor are mine to him.

Alberto just passed by. "If you are writing to Luke," he said, "tell that boy that the fences we built together are the best in all the valley—and the mules are missing him."

I never supposed that my feelings would be shared by eighteen mules.

Ever and fondly,
Eldora

---

adobe. Sun-dried brick made of silt. Also used to refer to buildings made of this material.

Alcott, Bronson. (1799–1888) Father of Louisa May Alcott, he was an idealistic educator, a social reformer, and cofounder of a cooperative vegetarian community.

apothecary. An individual's supply of medicinals or, as in present usage, a store where they are sold.

aqua fortis. Now known as nitric acid. A liquid with powerful corrosive properties, it is used in etching steel or copper and in the manufacture of explosives and dyestuffs.

camino real. The Spanish word *real* has two syllables: *re*, as in "reason," and *al*, as in "Alfred." It means "royal." Thus, the *camino real* is the Royal Road.

carreta. Small cart with heavy wooden wheels, generally pulled by a single ox.

catarrh. An inflammation of the mucous membranes of the nose and throat, causing a heavy cough. It was not uncommon in the nineteenth century and could worsen into pneumonia, an often fatal disease before antibiotics were discovered. The stress is on the second syllable; the *h* and the two *r*'s are pronounced as one.

claim jumper. Person who seizes land already claimed by another.

dinner. The main meal of the day, taken at midday. Supper, at day's end, was lighter. Breakfast was often large and hearty, sometimes postponed until the first chores of the day had been completed.

fair copy. After all corrections of manuscripts, letters, and other documents had been satisfactorily completed, a carefully written fair copy was prepared in anticipation of sending to others or of publication.

fisticuffs. Fighting with bare fists; punching.

flapjacks. Pancakes made on a frying pan or a griddle with a slightly raised edge. Flapjacks are so called because they are turned by being tossed into the air and then caught back on the pan so that the second side is cooked.

going to see the elephant. Nineteenth-century expression having the meaning of expecting something new and exciting; possibly a reference to the excitement generated when circuses first acquired elephants and paraded them upon arriving in town.

kettle. Large container used to boil liquids, cook food, etc. A tea kettle is distinguished by its spout.

millrace. Channel in which water driving a mill wheel flows to the mill.

pies. Practical and popular meals-in-one. They were not a fruit-filled dessert item, but consisted of meat, vegetables, or both enclosed in a pastry crust.

sandbar. A ridge of sand formed along the banks of a river by the action of its current.

Sandwich Islands. Former name of Hawaii.

San Pedro. The San Pedro of the story is a fictional settlement, loosely based on San Juan Bautista although it lacks that city's landmark mission. It should not be confused with California's actual San Pedro, which is southwest of the Salinas Valley.

wainwright. One who makes and repairs wagons.

LIST OF ILLUSTRATIONS

Page 1, Chapter I. *Galvanized Iron House.* (Drawing.)
Courtesy of the Huntington Library.

Page 65, Chapter II. *Mining Methods of Early Days.*
(Drawing.) Courtesy of the Bancroft Library
(#F861.C87).

Page 111, Chapter III. *California Landscape.* (Drawing.)
Courtesy of the Mariposa Museum and History Center.

Page 157, Chapter IV. *Bowie Knife.* (Drawing.) Courtesy of
the Mariposa Museum and History Center.

Page 189, Chapter V. *Numerals Written by Child.* Courtesy
of the author.

Page 229, Chapter VI. *Castro-Breen Adobe.* (Note: This
building is fictionalized as the posada of the story.)
Copyright © 1938 by California State Parks.

Page 261, Chapter VII. *California: General View of the
City of San Francisco in 1850.* Copyright © 2007 by
Bettmann/CORBIS.

Page 306, Glossary. *Iron Kettle.* (Drawing.) Courtesy of the
Mariposa Museum and History Center.

ABOUT THE AUTHOR

JOAN W. BLOS won the 1980 Newbery Medal and the American Book Award for Children's Fiction for *A Gathering of Days*, a work of historical fiction and her first novel. She is the author of *Brothers of the Heart*, which continues that story, and of *Brooklyn Doesn't Rhyme*, a novella for somewhat younger children. Her fourteen picture books include *The Heroine of the Titanic*, an award-winning title, *Old Henry*, illustrated by Caldecott medalist Stephen Gammell, and *Martin's Hats*, illustrated by Caldecott medalist Marc Simont. A native New Yorker, she lives in Ann Arbor, Michigan.

*For their help and encouragement I wish to thank
Tom Burnett, Zibby Oneal, Herb Kaufer, and Sarah Blos;
also the patient and resourceful staff of the Reference
Desk of the Harlan Hatcher Library of the University
of Michigan; and special thanks to Clarence Brown for
offering the use of his name.*